Lydia's Journey

Lydia's Journey

An
Armenian
Refugee's
Story

Katherine Covell

Somewhat Grumpy Press Inc.

Published by arrangement with Somewhat Grumpy Press Inc. Halifax, Nova Scotia, Canada.
www.SomewhatGrumpyPress.com
The Somewhat Grumpy Press name and logo are registered trademarks.

ISBN
978-1-7387998-0-0 (paperback)
978-1-7387998-1-7 (eBook)

First Printing, May 2023

CONTENTS

Prologue   1

1   4

2   8

3   12

4   15

5   18

6   22

7   26

8   31

9   36

10   42

Part Two

11   48

CONTENTS

12 | 52

13 | 56

14 | 61

15 | 66

16 | 71

17 | 75

18 | 79

Part Three

19 | 84

20 | 88

21 | 93

22 | 98

23 | 102

24 | 107

25 | 111

26 | 116

27 | 121

28 | 125

29 | 130

30 | 134

31 | 139

32 | 144

33 | 148

34 | 152

35 | 157

36 | 163

Part Four

37 | 170

38 | 174

39 | 179

40 | 184

41 | 188

42 | 193

43 | 197

CONTENTS

44 | 202

45 | 207

Epilogue 212

AUTHOR'S NOTE 217
ACKNOWLEDGEMENTS 219
ABOUT THE AUTHOR 221

In memory of my parents, Lydia Krikorian and Boghos Haratounian. Photo courtesy Karen Sarkissian.

It was late in the afternoon in Constantinople when the Minister of the Interior called the meeting to order. It had been two months since he had proposed deporting the remaining Armenians from the region. So far, he had got rid of only the elite. Several hundred Armenian intellectuals had been executed.

"We are here," he told the local governor and the soldiers who were seated around the table, "to settle the Armenian question once and for all. For too long, these dreadful Christians have made demands on us; they have complained about their taxes, and they have demanded rights. We must make sure they relinquish such revolutionary ambitions. Despite our earlier efforts, they remain a danger to our state. This danger must be eliminated," he proclaimed. "And it must be now, now, now," he stressed. "Not only do their demands continue, but these infidels are daring to help the Russians against us and our German allies. Enough!" he shouted, slamming his fist on the table. "We shall stop them. This time, we will do a thorough job. There is only one way in which we can defend ourselves against them in the future, and that is just to deport them. Through the desert we'll lead them." He grinned. "We will start in earnest tomorrow in Zeitun. Now let us talk details."

Part One

Zeitun to Aleppo

1915 –1918

1

"So, if you were Noah," Lydia Zakarian asked her six-year-old brother, "and there was a big flood coming, which animals would you put in the ark to save?"

"Dinosaurs." Luke replied without hesitation.

"Don't be silly Luke," she laughed, "they'd be too big to get in and they'd take up too much space."

"But I wouldn't let them drown in the flood. Did Noah? Where would they go? Can dinosaurs swim?" Luke asked. Lydia giggled.

Their mother, Mayda, smiled as she listened to her children's chatter. The three of them sat at the kitchen table. Lydia, her long dark hair framing her face, was drawing two donkeys walking into Noah's ark on her sketch pad while chatting with Luke. Luke, with the same large brown eyes and shiny black hair as his sister, was sculpting a T-Rex from salt dough. Mayda was peeling and dicing onions. Tonight, they would have a family favourite, cabbage dolmas stuffed with lamb, rice, and onions.

Ever since she had heard the story of Noah's ark at Sunday school, ten-year-old Lydia had been full of questions about the animals. She wanted to know which animals were allowed onto the ark, how Noah looked after them all, and what happened when they landed on Mount Ararat. Did they march two by two into Yerevan, she had asked.

"Would you like to help me squeeze the lemons for the dolmas?" Mayda asked the children.

"I will," Lydia replied, picking up a wedge of lemon. "I can mix the rice and meat, too. Mum," she continued, "could we go to Yerevan and see where Noah landed? Is the ark still there?"

"That would be fun, wouldn't it? But it's a long way from here and it would take us many days to get there."

"He should have brought the animals to Zeitun. We have lots of mountains," Luke added, "then I could check for dinosaur bones."

"Maybe Noah thought it was too hilly here for all the animals, and there were no dinosaurs silly, so there wouldn't be any bones. Isn't that right?" Lydia asked her mother.

Mayda smiled and continued wrapping the lamb mixture into cabbage leaves. She treasured these times with her children. She hoped they would continue. The children had always been happy and got along well. Their life in Zeitun was good. The sound of the nearby river running was soothing, and the high mountains surrounding the valley felt protective. But she was anxious about their future and no longer felt safe.

The Ottoman Empire had entered the war six months earlier, and it was allied with Germany. Mayda knew that the Armenian community was helping the Russians against the Turks. At first, after discussing her concerns with community leaders and her husband, Daron, she had felt reassured that Zeitun's turbulent past would not be repeated. Then things changed.

Many Armenian civil servants had been dismissed from their positions by the Young Turks. A couple of weeks ago, some local Armenians, including a priest and a teacher she knew, had been arrested. There had been talk of deportation, and the previous day, their wonderful monastery burned to the ground. The smoke and the smell were as distressing as they were pervasive. Lydia had been upset by the fire and asked her what had happened. Mayda was unsure how to respond. She prayed it was an accident and not a harbinger of things to come. She reminded herself that it was mostly the political and religious community leaders, and a few outspoken individuals who had been arrested. As a merchant family, surely, they would be safe. Surely there would be no deportations. It was unthinkable.

Her parents had told her all about the first resistance in 1862, when the Sultan had tried to take control of the region. They were shocked that it happened again in 1895. Her older brother and her uncle were among the many who had been killed when the Armenians, fearing a massacre, had mounted an armed defence against the Ottoman Empire during the so-called second resistance. Mayda had been a teenager then. She could not imagine Lydia having to experience a similar upheaval in her teen years.

She shuddered as she recalled the horrors of the time, and silently gave thanks to God that her children had been born well after the conflict ended. Surely it could not happen for a third time, she thought. There were so few Armenians left in Zeitun. Why would the Turks bother? And surely the war would end soon. Sighing, she wrapped the last dolma.

"Dad will be closing up the store now," she told the children, as she layered the dolmas side by side in a large saucepan. "Why don't you two go play outside 'til dinner's ready. Luke, you can clean up the play dough, and then put your dinosaur on the table in the living room."

Daron had been running the general store since their marriage twelve years earlier. He stocked a wide variety of food but specialized in local produce. The figs, grapes, and olives, which he grew with Madya's help, were legendary in the local community. The Zakarians were fortunate to have a large lot behind the store and a comfortable house beside it.

Mayda heard Daron come in. They kissed and Daron, sniffing the redolent aroma, gave his wife a hug. "I do love you, Mayda," he said, grinning, "but most of all when you make dolmas. Are they ready? I'm hungry."

The children were called in. They washed their hands and sat at the table with their parents. It was Lydia's turn to say grace. They reached around the table to hold hands while Lydia thanked God for the food, her parents, her brother, and for helping Noah save the animals. She continued, "And please God, can you make sure nothing else in our town burns like our monastery did because," she paused. Before she could complete the sentence, the rest of the family ended the prayer with a loud "Amen." The dolmas were waiting, and they were hungry.

2

Waking, Mayda noticed that the smell of the burned monastery remained strong. She wondered how many priceless ancient manuscripts had gone up in smoke. But it was Saturday, and the sun was shining. She was determined to enjoy the day without undue worry. Daron was already up and dressed. The store was always busy on Saturdays, and he needed to get there early. She checked on the children. Lydia was sitting up in her bed and reading her book of Bible stories. Luke was still asleep.

Mayda thought about her plans for the day as she prepared breakfast. Saturdays were traditionally clothes washing day, but she had washed hers yesterday. She wanted to be free this Saturday to work on the dress she was making for Lydia. Mayda wondered if her sister would need help with her laundry. She could send Lydia to help her Aunt Ruth. Ruth, Mayda's younger sister, was seven months pregnant with her first child. She could use the help, and Lydia always enjoyed spending time with her aunt. But Mayda would make sure that Lydia also had time to practice her violin.

There was a concert scheduled the next weekend at Lydia's school. Mayda and Daron were very proud when they learned Lydia had been chosen to play a solo. Lydia would be playing Beethoven's "Ode to Joy." She had learned from her teacher that it was based on a poem by Schiller and that it represented hope, unity, and peace among all peoples. She had told her mother what she learned. On hearing this, Mayda thought it particularly apt and timely. It also made her realize why it was one of her favourite pieces. It always calmed her, and she had noticed that Lydia seemed to fall into a dreamlike state when she played it. She hummed it to herself as she set the table.

Mayda hoped to finish Lydia's concert dress before dinner time. She had found a bolt of pale blue satin from which she had made a dress with a full skirt and puffed sleeves. The finishing touch would be the wide band of dark blue ribbon, which she would stitch around the waistline, leaving enough to tie a large bow at the centre. She would cut strips of the ribbon to tie bows at the ends of Lydia's braids. Lydia, she thought, would look as lovely as her music sounded.

Mayda sniffed. She could still smell burning. It upset her, but, looking out the window, there was no sign of any further fires or damage. Just a few wisps of smoke hung over the rubble of the monastery. Maybe it really was just an accident, she thought.

"Mum," asked Lydia, as she came into the kitchen, "can I go play with Sarah today?"

"Well, first you should practice for your violin solo, and then I was hoping that you wouldn't mind helping your Aunt Ruth with her laundry. Then, if you like, you could invite Sarah to stay here for dinner with us."

"Okay, mum, thanks."

"Would you call your dad and brother for breakfast now?"

* * *

Mayda cleaned up from breakfast, then took Lydia's almost finished dress out and laid it across the table. She had a hem to finish on one sleeve and then she would stitch the ribbon sash on. She could hear Lydia practising in her room. Lydia enjoyed playing her violin, but she really wanted to learn to play the oud like her Uncle Sahag. Maybe, Mayda thought, they could purchase an oud for her next birthday. She wondered what the Beethoven piece would sound like on the oud. Lydia seemed destined for a brilliant future. She was talented musically, she excelled in her schoolwork, and she was well liked by her teachers and other students.

As for Luke, Mayda thought, acknowledging her bias to herself, he was the sweetest and kindest little boy she had ever come across. He was always ready to help others and was truly upset if he saw a hurt animal or bird. He had gone to the store with Daron. Luke could help stock the shelves and liked it when his dad would let him serve some customers. That always made him feel important and grown-up.

* * *

Lydia found her Aunt Ruth at the first of a row of washtubs along the river. There were other neighbourhood women washing clothes as well. Lydia waved and smiled at each of them as she approached Ruth. Ruth was standing in her slip and bare feet. Her dress and stockings were in the washtub.

"Hello Auntie," Lydia said, "I've come to help you." Ruth turned her attention from the washtub to her niece. Lydia noticed that Ruth's abdomen was moving. "Is that the baby kicking you, Auntie? I think I see it. Can I put my hand on your tummy and see if I can feel him?" Lydia was enchanted.

"Of course you can Lydia—but why 'him'? Do you think this baby is a boy?"

"Yes, and I think you should call him Noah."

Ruth smiled. "I'm not sure what your Uncle Sahag would think of that," she said. "He wants to name the baby Boghos if it is a boy. But I'll ask him about Noah when I...." She stopped speaking and gasped as she looked beyond Lydia. A look of terror replaced her smile. Lydia, confused, looked behind her.

Three soldiers with guns drawn and whips at their sides were approaching the women.

"Move, go. NOW." The soldier yelled at them both as he approached, cracking his whip on the ground beside them. "You are not safe here. You must leave."

"Please sir," Ruth's voice wavered, "I need my clothes and shoes. What is happening? Where are we to go? I cannot leave my husband. You can see, sir, I soon will have a baby."

"And I can't go anywhere without my parents' permission," Lydia said firmly. "I have to let them know where I am going." She turned back to the washtub.

The soldiers laughed. "We have a bright one here, eh? We shall have fun with her. Remember the Pasha told us we could do as we please with the women and girls."

"Move." A soldier pushed at them with the butt of the gun, laughing. "Just move along."

Confused, semi-clad and barefoot, Ruth was pushed along. Lydia clung to her hand. A stream of women in similar states of distress followed them. They left a trail of shoes and wet clothing strewn across the riverbank.

3

The soldiers marched the women alongside the river Shugur and down the steep hillside. Lydia noticed that, like her Aunt Ruth, many of the women were barefoot and carried nothing. As they approached the bottom of the hillside, Lydia saw a long column of Zeitunis being marched out of town. Soldiers pushed Lydia, her aunt, and the other women into the column. It grew longer as they were marched past the remaining homes in the city. By the time they reached the city limits, it seemed to Lydia that almost every resident of Zeitun, at least the women, must be in the group.

"Aunt Ruth," she asked, "what is happening? There are so many people here. Where are we being taken, where is my family, what is happening to us?"

"I don't know Lydia. Just hold my hand and keep walking. We'll watch for your parents and Luke and your Uncle Sahag."

Lydia tried to focus solely on keeping walking. With a great deal of determination and fortitude, she kept her focus on the path ahead and repeated to herself, left foot, right foot, left foot, right foot. They continued. Hoping to locate her family, Lydia kept looking around as she walked. She noticed that a few people seemed to be carrying packages of food. It had been a while since she had breakfast and she was hungry. She recognized a girl from her class at school, carrying her infant sister. She saw a few older men who, like some of the children, were struggling to keep up. She did not see her family. They walked on.

Lydia heard whips cracking and men shouting. She heard the steady thump of boots. She heard babies and children crying. She heard dogs barking. She heard people begging God to help them. One older man beside Lydia plaintively called out, "Why, why, why, why." She wished he would stop. She was trying hard to stay strong and not cry. Lydia tightened her grip on Ruth's hand. She heard her heart hammering loudly. She watched in horror as one woman tried to run from the column. The soldiers shouted at her to stay in the line. One hit her across the legs with his whip. She was panting and sobbing. She fell.

"We must do as they say," Ruth cautioned Lydia. "Keep hold of my hand, stay quiet, and keep walking. We'll stay together and we'll be all right."

"Keep up and keep quiet child, like she told you," said an older woman who was walking beside Ruth. "You better hold on to that child," she said to Ruth in a low voice, "I recognize some of the men who are holding the guns—they are criminals, murderers. I heard a rumour that Talat Pasha had ordered them to be released from prison to become merciless killers of us Armenians. They apparently were told they could drown us, throw us off cliffs, or burn us alive. Not the beautiful young girls, of course, like your little girl—they will be kept for raping. It is unbelievable." Lydia had not heard all that was said, but Ruth's ashen face and trembling body worried her.

"Aunt Ruth, look, we are at the edge of town. Where do you think they are taking us now?" Before Ruth could answer, the column stopped and the men in it were ordered to stand aside. Lydia looked carefully. She thought she saw her Uncle Sahag, but when the man turned around, she realized it wasn't him. She could see neither her father nor her brother among the men. Her disappointment turned to relief as the men's hands were tied and they were led away. Shots rang out. The soldiers returned alone. Lydia could no longer quell the tears. Trembling and sobbing, they walked on.

* * *

Day after day, and then week and week, Lydia and Ruth walked. The days were long and difficult. They never stopped feeling as though they were living a nightmare. Each day they looked for Mayda and Luke among the hundreds of women and children.

They did not know where they were being taken. They did not know why they were being taken. They knew only that their numbers were dwindling. Each day, some were robbed, raped, killed, or died from disease, starvation, or suicide. Each day, they wondered if it would be their last.

The route they were led on could have been easier. But the soldiers who controlled the group kept the women and children away from villages and population centres as much as possible. Instead of using the main routes, they marched them on circuitous paths through narrow mountain passes and across rivers toward the Syrian desert. Food and water were always in scant supply. Whatever food a few of the deportees had brought with them had long been eaten or stolen. Occasionally they were able to get some bread from a small village or farm they passed, but hunger and thirst were with them always. The thirst was most acute during the scorching daytime sun, the hunger during the cold and damp nighttime hours. Their strength was diminishing.

Lydia tried to stay strong for Ruth. She knew that Ruth increasingly had been struggling to keep up. It was clear to Lydia that Ruth was exhausted, and that she desperately needed rest and nutrition. Several of the older women, other pregnant women, and some infants had died of starvation during the past days. Their bodies were left by the roadside. Others had been stripped naked and forced to walk in the scorching sun until they dropped dead. Lydia worried Ruth might soon be among the dead. The psychological toll was as great as the physical toll.

They walked in silence. Neither spoke of the rape of a young woman they had witnessed the previous evening. Neither spoke of the elderly women who were shot because they lagged behind the group. Neither spoke of the woman in front of them who was shot when she fell. Neither spoke of the pregnant woman who had delivered by the side of the road that morning and then died of a hemorrhage, the baby left to die as well. But the images haunted them as they trudged on.

4

The next day started like so many previous on the march. Soldiers forced the surviving women and children, exhausted, starving, and dehydrated, to rise at daybreak and continue the march. Some of the soldiers stood by, mocking the women's and girls' skeleton-like emaciated bodies. As on previous days, there were voluntary and involuntary drownings, indiscriminate killings, rapes, and abandoned corpses.

Hours later, as they trudged under the scorching noonday sun, one of the soldiers who was leading the caravan stopped it and told the women and children that they were in imminent danger of an attack from a gang of Kurds.

"Leave everything here," he shouted. "That will appease them, and you will be safe." The women dropped what few items they had, grabbed the children, and ran as much as was possible into the brush. The soldiers themselves ran off. The Kurds came.

In the ensuing panic, Lydia and Ruth were separated. Lydia hid behind a rock from where she could see some of the attackers gleefully gather up the few possessions that had been left behind. She could not see Ruth. She watched in horror as a small boy, who had become separated from his mother as they ran, fell. He got up and tried to run on. He was grabbed by a Kurdish rebel, stripped naked, and hurled into the river. Lydia heard the anguished screams of the boy's mother. She watched helplessly as the boy's mother jumped into the river after her son. She saw some of the elderly marchers being beaten, and some shot. Their clothes and the few possessions they still had, if any, were taken. Their bodies were left naked to burn in the heat of the sun. She saw young women being raped. Lydia crouched lower. She closed her eyes. She prayed Ruth was safe. She prayed that her parents and brother Luke were safe, and her schoolfriend Sarah. She wondered where they all were. She wished at least one of them was with her.

After what seemed to her like many hours, Lydia heard the soldiers return and call those left in the caravan to get moving. Tentatively, and afraid of what she might see, she emerged from her hiding place. To her immense relief and joy, it was only a few moments before she saw Ruth. Ruth had survived the attack. Many had not. Picking her way carefully among the corpses, Lydia ran to her. Ruth clasped her. They were both sobbing quietly.

"I have to rest now Lydia; I just can't go on," Ruth said shortly after they resumed walking. "You go on with the others. Anoush Levonian will take care of you. You remember her, don't you? She lives next door to us. I saw her after the attack. I think she is just up ahead a bit—you go catch up to her. You will be safe with her."

"No Auntie, I'll help you." Lydia was emphatic. "I won't leave you. You must keep going." Lydia pleaded. "We must find my parents and Luke and Uncle Sahag. They must be with another group; we will find them. We must. Come on Auntie, you can."

As they walked, Lydia saw that Ruth's feet were swollen and had numerous cuts on them.

"You need some shoes, Aunty," she said. "And I'm going to get you some." She had been observing the soldiers and had identified one who seemed less cruel than most. She went up to him. "My aunt needs some shoes," she told him. "And I would like you to find her some." The soldier was amused by Lydia's boldness. He did not answer her, but he removed a pair of sandals from the feet of one of the many corpses that lined the path.

"Here," he said gruffly to Lydia. "Take these to your aunt. This woman has no need for them. Your aunt can wear them."

Ruth was both surprised and grateful. Although a poor fit, the sandals made walking easier than it had been barefoot. But even with the sandals, it remained a gruelling trek. Ruth was spent. She stopped and leaned on Lydia. She could no longer hide her fear. "I am worried about this baby, Lydia. I feel that it is almost ready to come. This is no place to have a baby. And what will happen—what will the soldiers do? Will they kill me? Will they kill the baby? Will we be attacked again? What will happen to us? You've seen how cruel they can be."

Lydia hugged Ruth. "I'll look after you and baby Noah, I promise. Please Auntie, keep walking." Ruth sighed. She forced a smile. They walked on slowly, arm in arm. Coming to a river, Lydia and Ruth waded in. They drank thirstily from the water before splashing it on their faces and over their heads. Lydia saw a young woman, who looked not much older than she, walk into the river until the water was over her head. Lydia thought she might be one of the women she had seen raped. Lydia watched as the woman slipped away in the current and did not surface. Ruth took Lydia's hand and led her away.

As they walked on, Lydia realized that Ruth, despite her efforts, may not be able to continue. She was walking more slowly and panting. She kept one hand on her abdomen as though holding the baby inside. Lydia was still determined to help Ruth keep going. She slackened her pace to match that of her aunt. As they walked, Lydia could feel Ruth writhing.

"Lean on me, Auntie," she said as she took Ruth's arm. "You have to keep going, please, please try." Lydia kept one arm around Ruth, trying to provide enough support to help Ruth continue walking. Lydia knew that if they lagged too far behind, they would be shot. The fact of Ruth's pregnancy would not stop an execution.

"Lydia," Ruth said, "I'm sure the baby will come soon. I'm really trying, but I don't think I'm going to be able to keep going. You must promise me that you will keep going if I stop or if I'm shot. You must leave me and save yourself. Find Anoush." Ruth's voice was fading as she sank to the ground. "I will be alright. Go child."

Lydia glared at her aunt. "No," she said. "I won't leave you and I won't leave baby Noah. I want to meet him!"

5

Night was falling, and the caravan was slowing when the first contraction hit. It was unmistakable. Ruth clutched her abdomen and groaned. "Lydia," she gasped, "the baby, I think it's coming. I can't...." She stopped as another contraction left her doubled over in pain.

Lydia looked around. She was nervous. No one was looking in their direction. There was no one to help. It was getting dark. Most of the women and children were settling down for the night. Lydia could see and hear the soldiers, but they were not looking in her direction. They were occupied with aiming their rifles at two elderly women who had collapsed by the side of the path a few moments earlier. Lydia heard one of the women pleading with them.

"Please sir, just let us sleep. We will be fine in the morning. We will not cause any trouble."

The soldier beside her laughed. "You know what happens to laggards like you? Pow—gone. You're old anyway, going to die soon, so why not now?" Placing his rifle against her chest, he cocked the hammer.

Lydia forced herself to look away and focus on her aunt. She needed to find a place for her aunt to lie down. She decided against the riverbank since there were already many others settling there. Lydia decided the safest place would be behind an unusually large rock she had seen earlier at a nearby bend in the river.

"Quick Auntie, get behind that rock while they aren't watching us. Quick! I'll help you."

Ruth crawled over. Lydia, noticing a twig on the ground, recalled her mother telling her that sometimes it helped to bite down on something if you were in pain. Her mother had been pulling a sliver from Lydia's finger. She knew little of the pain of childbirth, but she could see her aunt's discomfort. She grabbed at the twig and gave it to Ruth. There could be no noise.

"Bite on this Auntie. It might help. Is there anything else I can do to help?" Lydia whispered. Ruth took Lydia's hand and tried to smile. Lydia could sense the fear Ruth was feeling despite the smile. She was also feeling her own.

"Can you find something wet? I am sweating, and I think it may get worse." Ruth whispered back as she writhed in pain. "Something cold and wet on my face would really help—if that's possible."

After ensuring that Ruth was well hidden and that the soldiers were still occupied with others, Lydia took her socks off and, crawling on her stomach to the river, she wetted them and crawled back. She used the wet socks to wipe the sweat from Ruth's face. She did not know what else to do.

A moment later, the quiet of the night was shattered by the loud pop-pop-pop sound of gunshots. They looked at each other without speaking. They knew that the two elderly women had been murdered. They knew that if the soldiers found Ruth behind the rock, it would be the end. Ruth would not be the first pregnant woman to be shot before or after giving birth. Hers would not be the first newborn thrown in the river. Lydia shuddered, but like her aunt, tried hard to focus on the immediate task. Could they—a first-time mother and a young girl—see a baby safely born in these horrendous circumstances? Lydia had missed her mother every moment of the march, but never more than she did now as she watched her aunt writhing in pain and biting hard on the twig. She needed to do something.

It was almost dark, but Lydia could see enough to gather some grasses and reeds and place them on the ground behind the rock. "It's kind of a bed," she whispered to Ruth. Ruth dragged herself onto the pile. Lydia peered around the rock. She saw the soldiers walking among the women and children. "Pretend you are asleep, Auntie," she whispered in Ruth's ear. "The soldiers are coming this way." Lydia laid still with her eyes closed. Biting harder on the stick, Ruth managed to stay still and silent. The soldiers stopped before they reached the area where Ruth and Lydia were hiding. They had found their prey.

A few moments later, the quiet of the night was again interrupted. This time by screams. Lydia cautiously peered around the rock. Despite the darkening sky, she could see that one soldier was holding a young woman down while the other raped her. No one intervened. Every member of the caravan knew by now any effort to help the girl would lead quickly to their being shot. Lydia felt sick and helpless. "Your turn," Lydia heard the one soldier say to another as he climbed off the woman's now still and completely naked body.

Lydia saw Ruth was too absorbed in her own pain to pay attention to the woman's screams. She watched Ruth writhing with more frequency. She watched the pain etched on Ruth's face.

"Bite harder" Lydia said, "you'll feel better. Here, take my hand." Lydia felt her hand squeezed so hard she thought the bones may break, but she stayed resolute. Her aunt would be okay. Baby Noah would be fine. Lydia peeked around the rock and was relieved to see the soldiers were nowhere near them. Ruth would not be able to stay quiet much longer. Lydia wiped the sweat from Ruth's brow with her free hand. She recalled the noise her mother made when she gave birth to Luke, and that was at home in bed.

"Lydia, help me take off my underwear. I think it's time." Lydia did so, her anxiety increasing, her confidence waning. The night darkened further. Lydia noticed a lizard slithering along the rock that was their refuge. From a distance came the sound of wolves howling. Neither slept. The night seemed endless. As the dawn was breaking, Lydia was more exhausted and more afraid than she had ever been. She continued to use her socks, now wet from the dew, to wipe the sweat from Ruth's face and neck. Ruth was continuing to writhe in pain. Just when neither thought they could last any longer, Ruth turned her face to Lydia.

"Now" she whispered. "I need to push now. Can you kneel between my legs and help?"

Lydia shook with fear, but she also felt excitement and relief that this might be over soon. She was terrified the soldiers would hear them and they would all be shot. She kneeled, wondering exactly what she was supposed to do. She focused on her aunt.

Ruth pushed her hands into the ground and arched her back, spreading her legs as widely as she could. She panted and grunted. Lydia watched in awe as first a head covered in black hair and then a small body emerged from between Ruth's legs. She instinctively caught the newborn but was puzzled by the cord which continue to tether it to Ruth. The baby mewled.

"She's alive." Ruth whispered with astonishment and happiness.

One more grunt, and Lydia saw what the cord was attached to. Ruth had expelled a disk-like shape of what looked like shiny flesh; its diameter was much larger than its thickness. Lydia recalled seeing such a thing a few times on the march when women had given birth. She was still not sure what it was. She quickly forgot about it in her delight that the baby was born, and her equal disappointment that it was not the Noah she had been expecting.

"Give her to me, Lydia." Ruth put the baby to her breast, hoping that the skin-to-skin contact would be soothing and keep her quiet.

"Lydia," she whispered, now feeling both happy and terrified, "meet your new cousin Ani. Ani was my grandmother's name. It means fighter, and I think that's what this little girl is going to be. Ani, this is your clever cousin Lydia. She will care for you. Now we must stay silent and get some sleep."

6

Less than two hours later, Lydia woke to the sound of a crying newborn and the heat of the sun burning her face. She immediately recalled the events of the night, sat up, and looked over at Ruth and baby Ani. Ruth was lying still. Her dress was matted with blood. Her skin was white. Over the past two weeks, Lydia had seen enough of death to recognize it. Ani was lying across Ruth's chest. Her legs were drawn up, her tiny fists were clenched, and her face was red. Lying on the ground beside her was the placenta, and a sharpened twig which Ruth had used to saw through the umbilical cord. The cord, Lydia noticed to her astonishment, was tied with intertwined pieces of grass and reeds.

A wave of panic swept over Lydia. She realized she could do nothing for Ruth. There was no way to bury her, and no time. Lydia forced herself to focus on the baby. Ani was still alive; she would save her. Calling for help, she knew, would cause her death and the death of baby Ani. Recalling her mother showing her how to hold Luke when he was a newborn, Lydia held Ani close. She put a finger in Ani's mouth, hoping that the baby would suck on it and quieten. It worked.

Lydia became dimly aware of the sounds of the caravan getting ready to march on. The soldiers were calling to the women and children to hurry, to get into line, to get moving. If she were to stay with the caravan, she would need to hurry. She was exhausted. She was confused. She was terrified. Taking a deep breath, Lydia tried to quell the panic she was feeling. She recalled what her aunt had said the previous day. "Anoush Levonian will take care of you." Of course, she thought, I must find Anoush. Anoush will know what to do with Ani.

"Come Ani" she said quietly, "we will join the others and find Anoush and you will be safe." Kissing the baby on the top of her head, Lydia cradled her against her skin inside her dress. Given the lack of food over the past three weeks, her dress easily buttoned up over Ani. She peered around the rock. No soldiers were close by. Supporting Ani with one arm and silently saying goodbye to her aunt, Lydia ran ahead.

Lydia had seen Anoush on the first day they had been marching, but not since. Lydia realized that since Anoush had been alone, she was likely well ahead of her. Walking with Ruth had kept Lydia near the end of the long caravan. For a moment, she wondered if Anoush had survived. Had she been raped and murdered, like so many of the women? Who would she turn to help for then? Pushing such thoughts from her mind, Lydia moved ahead as quickly as she could without attracting attention.

Anoush was finishing her meagre allowance of bread and water when Lydia caught up with her later that morning. Signalling her to be quiet, Lydia opened the top buttons of her dress to reveal Ani. Anoush gasped. "Ruth's," Lydia whispered, and explained what had happened. "I think she is hungry and thirsty, and I have nothing to give her. Please help me, I don't know what to do." She started to cry. "I had to leave Auntie Ruth, Anoush." Lydia sobbed uncontrollably. "She's dead."

"Shush Lydia. There's nothing you could have done, but if you keep that up, we will both be shot, and baby Ani will be killed. Yesterday I saw three babies killed. Please, child, hold you sobs."

With one arm around Lydia, Anoush dipped her finger into the water she was drinking and put it in the baby's mouth. Ani sucked vigorously. Anoush looked as worried as Lydia felt. "We cannot let the soldiers see this baby. They'll probably throw her in the river like they have others." She said to Lydia. "Try to keep her hidden as you have and try to keep her quiet by holding her close to you. Keep walking beside me. I know you are tired, but we can't afford to attract attention. Let me think of what we can do."

Lydia, with tears running down her face, determinedly hummed "Ode to Joy" quietly as she walked along rubbing the baby's back. She thought it might help. She prayed Ani would stay silent. Lydia had never experienced such fear and confusion. Her heart was racing and she was sweating. She had not eaten or had any water for almost twenty-four hours and had little sleep. She felt shaky and struggled to keep walking through the rugged terrain. It was getting harder to hold on to the baby. She forced herself to continue humming. It helped. Anoush put her arm around Lydia. She slowed their pace to put them further back among the marchers where there were fewer soldiers. They walked in silence, carefully watching the soldiers, desperate not to be noticed. Ani, tucked well inside Lydia's dress, slept.

"Listen, Lydia," Anoush said quietly, some time later. "What do you hear?" Lydia stopped. The distant ringing of bells filled them both with hope. They had heard a similar sound the previous week and knew it meant a herd of goats was nearby. The sound got louder as they navigated the mountain pass.

Walking around a hairpin bend in the path, they came across a goatherder driving a large herd across the narrow path in front of them. The marchers and soldiers who were in front of the herd had continued and were out of sight. The rest of the caravan was stopped. There was nothing the soldiers could do to speed the animals across the path which wound steeply down the hillside to the valley below. Realizing that the terrain made escape impossible, and that it would take time for the herd to pass, the soldiers who had been scattered among the marchers gathered at the back to rest. Lydia quickly realized that she and Anoush were unguarded. She had an idea.

After ensuring that the soldiers were not able to see her, Lydia went up to the goatherder. She told him she was caring for a baby and begged him for some milk. Looking skeptical, he asked to see the baby. Moving the top of her dress, Lydia allowed him a glimpse of Ani. He gasped. He scratched his beard and thought for a moment.

"I won't give you milk," he said, "but if the baby is healthy, I'll take it. My wife has been wanting one. She cannot have a baby herself. Is it a girl? She'd love a little girl."

Lydia and Anoush were stunned and speechless. "Hurry and decide. I got to finish moving these goats along," he said. "Are you going to give me that baby or let her starve to death? It's up to you."

7

Lydia was traumatized by the loss of her Aunt Ruth and baby Ani. As they stumbled along, Lydia continually sought reassurance from Anoush that she had made the right decision. It had taken little more than a minute for Lydia to hand over the newborn. When she saw the smile on the goatherder's face as he looked down at the baby he was now cradling, she sensed Ani would be all right. Nonetheless, Lydia could not help feeling that she had let her aunt down and she cried, quietly. She cried for herself, her family, her aunt, and for baby Ani.

With each passing day, it became increasingly clear to both Lydia and Anoush that the goatherder had been the only hope for Ani. The number of children in the group was lessening. Many had died of heat stroke, some of dysentery, and many more from starvation. She realized how close Ani had come to being one of them. She imagined the goatherder and his wife feeding and playing with Ani. That image provided some relief. Lydia decided they had done the right thing.

Lydia and Anoush had seen many infants abandoned or killed by their desperate mothers. They had seen many women drown their children and themselves in the river. They had seen mothers lay their weakened mewling infants on a rock and walk on without them staring into space.

Lydia had almost learned to ignore the corpses that littered the path. She had learned to ignore the bodies that floated down the river or washed up on the banks. Ignoring the intense and endless hunger had become more difficult than ignoring the corpses. Lydia was desperate for food and water. It had been many days since they had passed any village.

The soldiers had kept what food was left for themselves. Anoush had shown Lydia how to pick seeds from animal manure and how to choose grasses that were edible. Lydia found it disgusting but quickly learned that seeds from dung were better than nothing and so she, like others, pounced greedily whenever she saw a pile of manure. These morsels were their primary diet. It was never enough. Like the other marchers, Lydia and Anoush became weaker and more exhausted. They could not have kept Ani alive. They were barely keeping themselves alive.

As they continued the march, they noticed more corpses along the side of the path, and in the river. Some were hanging among tree branches. Many were little more than skeletons.

"What's happening, Anoush?" Lydia asked. Although now used to corpses, the ones hanging in the trees were particularly grotesque and hard to ignore.

"I don't know, but I am wondering if there have been other groups ahead of us," Anoush commented. "There are so many more bodies here. Maybe there have been other caravans passing through here. But so many dead. So many skeletons. God help us."

"I'm so scared." Lydia said, clutching Anoush's hand. "Do you think my mother is still alive and will I ever see her again, or are we all going to die?" Lydia asked. "Maybe we should give up?"

"I don't know Lydia, I just don't know, but I pray that we live and that we find your family. So, child, we must keep going. Don't give up."

Late that evening, they came upon a large, chaotic encampment. There were several tents scattered throughout the camp, but most of the hundreds of women and children in the camp were sitting or lying on the ground with no protection. Many looked gaunt and sunburned. Some were naked. Many were sobbing. Some were sitting and gazing ahead as if in a comatose state. Others were laying down using rocks for pillows. But they were alive. Several soldiers were walking among them. After exchanging greetings with the guards at the camp, the soldiers who had accompanied the marchers left.

The soldiers at the camp ordered the new arrivals to sit in a small unoccupied area on the edge of the camp between some tents and the river. Exhausted from the endless walking over the past weeks, and emotionally drained from their experiences, they sat. It was crowded and uncomfortable. The sights and sounds around them were disturbing. But the sound of the river and the sight of the tents were comforting. Lydia hoped they could stay awhile. Even a few days without walking would be a welcome relief. She wondered if her mother or brother were at the camp. She decided she would look for them in the morning.

"Come Lydia, it's late. Let's see if we can get some sleep. Maybe they'll give us some food in the morning." Anoush cleared some rocks from the space she and Lydia occupied. They rested together beside a tent. Others sat or lay around them. Lydia shuddered as she heard a soldier walking toward them.

"Wouldn't want her," Lydia heard him scoffing at a young woman who lay naked on the ground. "She's too skinny and ugly." They laughed, and the soldier kicked at the woman's buttocks. "Let's find a better looking younger one. I could use some exercise tonight."

Lydia shrank against Anoush, turning her head. She pretended she was invisible. Anoush held her closely until her sobs subsided, and she fell asleep. Despite her exhaustion, Lydia's sleep was fitful, disturbed by confusion, fear, and hunger. The sleep of all was disturbed by screams and sobbing.

Waking at dawn, Lydia and Anoush were early enough to be among the few who received a slice of bread from the soldiers. They savoured every mouthful. Later that morning, they heard sounds and saw several carriages arriving at the encampment. They watched as well-dressed women emerged from the carriages and picked their way gingerly among the women and children, asking, "Are there any children for sale? Any children here—children for sale?"

Approaching Anoush, one woman pointed to Lydia. "Is she for sale?" she asked. "Look at her, so thin and sad looking, but still quite pretty. I'll buy her—she can help me around the house, and I will feed her and get her a decent dress. She looks like she needs caring for. Yes, I'll take her. How much do you want for her?"

Anoush put her arm around Lydia, who was shaking with fear. "Never will I sell this child."

"But," the woman continued, "looks like she will just starve to death here. Let me take her and you will give her a chance to live. I told you, I will take care of her. Don't you want to help her?"

"Lydia?" Anoush looked at her questioningly. "I won't go. Please don't make me." Lydia answered without hesitation, holding on to Anoush. Sighing, the woman moved on.

A few moments later, they saw the same woman leaving the camp with two girls who looked to be around six or seven years old. She put them into her carriage. As the carriage began to move, they heard someone shouting, "My children, my children, bring back my children!" They recognized her as one of the women who had marched with them from Zeitun. She was running after the carriage as it left the encampment. The carriage did not stop. She fell to the ground, screaming. Anoush and Lydia went over to her and tried to comfort her. She was inconsolable. The last of the carriages left; she still lay on the ground.

"I can't lose my children," she sobbed. "I thought they should be safe, but as soon as I saw them leaving, I knew I had made a terrible mistake. Oh, what have I done? What have I done? God forgive me. What shall I do? I cannot live without them. I have no reason to live without them."

Anoush tried her best to comfort the distraught woman After a few moments, she stopped sobbing. But she was not comforted. She stood up and pushed Anoush aside. Then, staring straight ahead, she walked into the river until she disappeared. Lydia trembled. She sank to the ground and covered her eyes with her hands. Anoush sat beside her and held her. Curling herself into the fetal position against Anoush, completely spent, Lydia fell asleep. Anoush stayed awake watching and holding her through the afternoon. She wondered how much more the child would have to endure.

Waking several hours later, just as the sun was setting, Lydia felt a hand stroking her hair. She opened her eyes and saw that Anoush was lying beside her, sleeping. Deciding she was dreaming, Lydia closed her eyes again. The stroking continued, and then she heard the gentle refrains of a woman humming the "Ode to Joy." Was it possible that she was not dreaming? Could it possibly be her mother?

8

The joy that Lydia and her mother experienced on finding each other was short-lived. Hugging her mother and sobbing, Lydia told her mother of the death of her Aunt Ruth and how she had tried to save the baby's life by giving her away. Mayda was devastated to learn of the loss of her sister and even more so of what her daughter had experienced. Her desire to protect her daughter had never been stronger nor more challenging.

Life in the open-air camp was brutal. Food was scarce and the only water available was from the river, which was also used for bathing and laundry. Disease was widespread. Death was commonplace. Local residents were allowed to enter the camp. Some brought in supplies to sell or barter. A few risked their lives to smuggle food and medications into the camp. But, more commonly, they came with ill intent. Every night, corrupt men from neighbouring communities raided the camp. The soldiers were complicit in allowing them to abduct or rape the girls and women. There were individual rapes and there were gang rapes. Most took place in the open. Sometimes the soldiers cheered them on. Sometimes the soldiers took part. Sexual violence and death were common nightly experiences.

Mayda had warned Anoush of what to expect when she first found her with Lydia. "Every night here, while we try to sleep," Mayda told Anoush, "Men come, they snatch young girls and do many bad things to them. Lydia cannot stay here. I must save her. I must act soon before she is defiled or killed."

"Have you heard anything about where they have taken our husbands and our sons?" Anoush asked Mayda. "They dragged me from beside the river and forced me to march with the others. I begged to see my family, but the soldiers just laughed."

"It was the same for me, Anoush. I was home alone after Lydia left to help Ruth with the laundry and Daron and Luke left for the store. I was almost finished making the dress for Lydia's recital. All I had left was sewing on the ribbon for the sash when I heard a very loud knocking at the door. I thought something might have happened to Lydia or Daron or Luke."

"You must have been frightened."

"I was, Anoush. Even more so when I opened the door. Two armed soldiers burst into our home, yelling at me to tell them who else was there. When I said there was only me, they pushed me aside and went through our home until they were sure there was no one hiding anywhere. Then they grabbed hold of me and dragged me out. I begged them to let me get some shoes on or a coat. I begged them to let me find my family first." Mayda paused and wiped a tear from her eye.

"It's okay, Mayda, you don't have to talk about it now."

"No. I want to." Mayda took a deep breath and continued. "They told me I had to go to Government House and to stop being foolish. Foolish! Pshaw! They shoved me into a long line of our neighbours being marched out of town. I looked for Ruth and Lydia as we passed the river. But all I saw were clothes and shoes."

"What about Daron and Luke?" Anoush asked. "Did you find out where they were?"

"Oh Anoush. I have not seen nor heard of them since they left for the store that morning. My darling husband and my beautiful son. I have prayed and prayed, but nothing Anoush. I can hardly bear it. All I can do now is whatever it takes to save Lydia."

The women hugged each other, both crying. "Let's try to get some sleep, Mayda, and we will find a way to save Lydia soon."

At night, the three slept together in a makeshift tent that Mayda had constructed. The tent was patched together with rags and scraps of clothing that she had removed from the dead. A few others had similar tents. Although rudimentary, the tents provided some protection from the cold dew, occasional rain, and from the attention of the soldiers and abductors. Mayda and Anoush slept, keeping Lydia cradled between them to keep her hidden. They were successful in protecting her, but every night Lydia heard the screams of those who were raped or were snatched and taken from their families and out of the camp. Often, the screams of mothers whose children had been taken were even louder and more prolonged than were those of their children.

The days were as challenging as the nights. Along with other women from Zeitun, Anoush, Mayda, and Lydia worked cooperatively to survive. They cared for the babies and children whose mothers had died, and they shared whatever food and water they could find. A few times a week they were given bread, but most of the time they subsisted on grasses. They were unsuccessful in their efforts to catch snakes or scorpions, but occasionally they shared a dead bird or animal. They remained hungry, thirsty, and exhausted. Survival strategies consumed most of their days.

The soldiers also delegated certain tasks to some women. Among these was the burying of corpses. Some women dug trenches which were to serve as communal graves. Others stripped the dead of whatever clothing they had left and placed the bodies in the trench. When the trench was full, the soldiers burned the bodies to make room for more. Anoush was assigned to the task of digging. Mayda was among those selected to remove the clothing from the dead. Each night, she thanked God that neither Lydia nor Anoush were among them. Each night, she feared it would not be long before they were all dead.

"Anoush," Mayda said, a few days after the reunion with her daughter and after their discussion about saving her, "we can wait no longer to save my daughter. I am going to have to get Lydia away from here now while she still has a chance of life. I don't think I can stand to watch her getting thinner and sadder each day, and there is so much sickness. And how much longer can we protect her at night? She may soon be raped or killed. I am not sure I can keep myself alive much longer. I must act while there is still some hope for her survival."

"It will be the hardest thing for you, but I think you're right. You could sell her to one of the soldiers here or to one of the villagers, perhaps a nice lady. I have heard that many think of Armenian girls as good for the Turkish nation—that they have strong and healthy babies. Despite having become so thin, Lydia is still a beautiful child, and she is at the age they like best. It is her best chance at survival. But of course, we will have to make sure she goes to a good family." Anoush sighed and wiped a tear from her cheek.

"Do you really think she would be okay? Do you think they would be kind?"

"Can it be any worse?" Anoush asked. "She is strong, but she has been through so much. As you said, it is unlikely that we can continue to keep her alive? What will happen to her when we die? Why don't you talk to her?"

Lydia was adamant. "I won't go without you. I won't leave you again." She clung to her mother.

"Come and sit beside me," Mayda said, "and let's talk about this." After an initial angry refusal, many tears, and two more days of fear and hunger, Lydia acquiesced. Mayda explained the realities of their situation in very general terms, and eventually convinced Lydia that the best hope for survival of them both was for her to go and live with a Turkish family. Anoush, who had been sitting with them, reminded Lydia that they had given Ani away to save her life. It had been hard, she stressed, but for the best. She was now safe and had a caring family. That's what they wanted for Lydia.

"After this is over," Mayda promised her, "I will find you and your brother, and your dad, and we shall be a family again. You will have your violin and we will get you an oud; we will make cheese boerags and cabbage dolmas." She smiled at Lydia. "You'll see. If I let you go now, that is possible. If not, we will both die. Sleep now. We will talk again later."

Two days later, when the soldiers came with some villagers to the camp, Lydia was among the older of the children being auctioned. She was the third to be sold to a local woman. The money would help Mayda and Anoush survive, unless it was stolen.

"God willing, she will be kind and Lydia will survive." Mayda said as she and Anoush stood together, their arms around each other, both sobbing as Lydia, bravely holding her head high, was among the large group of children led from the camp.

9

Lydia fumed on the journey between the camp and the Aydin's home. She could not believe that her mother had sold her, as though she were a goat. She recalled her mother's promise that they would be together again soon and tried hard to accept her situation. But she was too angry. Not only had her own mother sold her, but then the woman who bought her and promised to be good to her, had sold her again as soon as they were on the perimeter of the camp. She was a girl, not an object on a shelf in a store like her dad's. And how would her mother be able to find her if she kept getting sold? Who were these new people who had purchased her? Why had they? Her thoughts fed her rage.

Yusuf and Fatma Aydin were delighted to have acquired a young slave girl. The price had been more than they had expected to pay, but that was to be expected since they arrived late and so had purchased her from an intermediary. They would make sure they had not wasted their money. They paid Lydia little attention on the ride from the camp, but as soon as they arrived at their home, they stripped her, washed her thoroughly, loused and washed her hair, and gave her a clean dress to wear. She felt good to be clean and in fresh clothes, but no less angry, and nervous about what might come next. Yusuf and Fatma indicated she should sit at their table.

"She looks respectable now," Yusuf said, "but looking good is not enough. We must teach her the ways of Islam. We will make her into a good Muslim so that we are never ashamed that she is with us."

"Glory be to Allah." Fatma responded with a smile. "Praise be to Allah."

Lydia sat quietly. She sensed they were discussing her, but could not understand what they were saying. She had learned a few Turkish words and phrases from the soldiers, but not enough to follow the conversation. She watched her purchasers, as she thought of them, smile at each other, and guessed they were pleased with their purchase. As they spoke, she identified the words Islam, Quran, and Allah. She wondered if they were talking about themselves or if they mistakenly thought she was Muslim.

Fatma pointed at her and said, "Baya." Lydia did not know what that meant.

Yusuf shook his head, glared at Fatma and, pointing to Lydia, said "Hayriye."

Lydia thought maybe they were trying to guess her name, so she pointed to herself and said firmly, "Lydia."

"No," was the immediate response from Yusef. "Hayriye. Hayriye."

Fatma left the room, returning a few minutes later with a slice of bread and a spoonful of yogourt. "Hayriye eat," she said, handing Lydia the plate. Despite her anger, Lydia enjoyed what seemed like the first real food she had eaten in as long as she could remember.

As she ate, Yusef again pointed to her, saying, "Hayriye."

Fatma nodded and added, "Hayriye good Turkish Muslim name. Not Armenian." Lydia, to her dismay, understood.

Over the next few days, Lydia showed her capacity to learn the language more fully. She learned that her new name meant auspicious and beneficial and that was what the Aydins expected her to be. She overheard Yusef saying, "We have made a good purchase, Fatma. Hayriye is strong. She will be useful for milking the cows and sheep, and for cleaning the house as we intended." Lydia learned also that she was to deny her heritage.

"Hayriye," Yusef turned to her, "you must never speak any language other than Turkish, and we will teach you the ways of Allah."

"You must learn the Quran, of course," agreed Fatma. "You belong to us, child, and must always be obedient. You understand Hayriye?"

Lydia nodded. She understood, but she could not imagine being obedient, adopting Islam or giving up Armenian.

Lydia wondered how and how quickly she could get away. She decided she would run away and find her mother as soon as she could. She would not wait for her mother to find her. Strengthened by her resolve, she felt less anxious. That night, her fourth with the Aydins, she slept.

The following morning, shortly after she finished her breakfast of yogourt, there was a knock on the door. Fatma welcomed in a woman carrying a small case. "Finally you are here," she said, "and here is Hayriye. You must do your job now to show she is ours and a member of our community."

Fatma sat Lydia on a chair and held her down while the woman tied her in place. She could not move. The woman then pulled some needles from her case and jabbed at Lydia's chin. Fatma watched.

Repeatedly piercing Lydia's chin, the woman made a series of dots and lines. She then took out a pot of lamp black and carefully rubbed some into each of the small holes she had made. The pain was excruciating. When she had filled each hole with lamp black, she wiped the tears from Lydia's face. But the woman was not finished. She repeated the piercing and dying to make a similar pattern of dots and lines between Lydia's eyes and then across one wrist. Only then did the woman stop and pack up her equipment. After exchanging a few words with the Aydins, she left. Fatma untied Lydia.

Lydia stayed in the chair. She was in intense pain, physically and emotionally. She could not bring herself to move. Fatma and Yusef left her alone. An hour passed and she still had not moved. Another hour passed while Lydia remained seated, stunned, and unmoving.

The painful tattooing left her with confusion, tremors, and intense fatigue. The Aydins eventually realized just how traumatized she was and led her to her sleeping place. They left her alone until the next morning. Over the next two weeks, the scabs that developed over the piercings healed. The trauma and shame Lydia felt at being tattooed stayed with her.

Lydia's decision to run away was changed by the tattoos. She was embarrassed by how she looked. She was afraid that the markings on her face and wrist, now blue, would mean rejection by other Armenians, perhaps even her mother. She decided to remain with the Aydins until she felt stronger. As soon as she did, she would leave. If she could not find her mother, or if her mother rejected her, she would care for herself. She would not become the Aydins' Muslim slave girl. She would not stay very long.

In the meantime, Lydia was compelled to spend her days in hard labour. She had insufficient food and rest, and she was not allowed to speak Armenian or use her name, but she was neither physically abused nor sexually assaulted, nor was she forced into marriage. The Aydins followed the Quran closely and believed that any form of abuse was not acceptable. Lydia coped by repeatedly telling herself that she was safe and soon she would run. She settled into a routine.

Fatma woke Lydia early every morning. "Come Hayriye, there is work to be done." Yusef had taught Lydia how to milk the cows and sheep, the chore that she must complete before she was given a slice of bread for breakfast.

Although tired and still sleepy when she was woken each morning, being with the animals was Lydia's favourite part of each day. She named them and spoke to them, telling them of the horrors she had experienced on the march, talking about the loss of her family, admitting to them just how angry she was about the tattoos, and how desperate she was to find her mother.

"Come on Zabel," she'd say to one of the cows, "say something other than moo."

She milked the cows and then the three ewes. It had taken more practice with the sheep than the cows, but she soon learned to hold and manipulate the udders such that the sheep were okay, and the milk expelled into the bucket. She came to love the sheep. With their brown faces and legs and rather fat tails, they reminded her of a stuffed toy Luke had when he was a baby. She wondered if these were the kind of sheep that Noah had taken on the ark. She wondered where Luke was, if he indeed was still alive.

Sometimes, after the milking was finished, Lydia helped make feta cheese by stirring the milk into yogourt. Most days, once the animals had been milked and fed, Lydia was busy with household cleaning and kitchen chores. During these times, she would be silently praying for rescue and reunion with her family. In the evenings, Yusef taught her Turkish, Islam, and read the Quran to her. After she went to bed, she would talk to herself in Armenian. She did not want to forget the words.

* * *

Over the next two years, Lydia's labour remained the same, but her meals, sleeping arrangements and relationship with the Aydins improved. Despite continuing to miss her parents and brother Luke, Lydia adapted to life with the Aydins. After her experiences during the march, she remained grateful that Yusef never touched her, and that Fatma had been kind and helpful when she started menstruating. She began to participate in Muslim observances and occasional feast days. The cows remained her faithful listeners as she talked to them constantly about how she was feeling, her bodily changes, and her concerns for her future. Her desire to run and her expectation that she could find her mother waned.

Toward the end of the third year, Lydia noticed that her favourite cow, Zabel, was spending a lot of time lying alone in the corner of the corral. She sat beside her, rubbing her face, and talking to her gently. As she did, she noticed that Zabel's eyes looked sunken and her ears droopy. She spoke to Yusef about her concerns.

"Yes Hayriye, you are right. I fear this cow is very sick."

Not too long after, two of the sheep stopped producing milk. Lydia realized it had been a challenging year for the Aydins. Not only were they losing the animals, but their recent crop had failed. Meals became smaller and plainer. Lydia overheard Yusef and Fatma discussing how they would cope. Fatma's eyes, when she looked at Lydia, reflected her desperation.

"Hayriye," she said. "Come here and sit down. Yusef has something to tell you."

"You have seen our problems, Hayriye." Yusef started. Lydia nodded. "I am afraid we are going to have to let you go. Even though you have been useful and we have grown fond of you, it is our only way forward."

10

Lydia could not believe what she was hearing. Let her go? What did that mean? She was free? Her first thought was that she could look for her mother. She soon learned that she was mistaken. She would not be freed. She would once again be sold. Lydia was distraught. Sold like an animal once again. The pain she felt was intensified when she heard Yusef offering her as "a well-assimilated, hardworking, and obedient Muslim girl."

She was helpless to stop the sale. After several hours of haggling, she was sold to another Turkish family for five sheep and one goat. Her buyer, Okan Yuvuz, was happy.

"My animals were a small price for you," he said to an enraged Lydia. "Look at you, a pure, beautiful, and strong young girl. And you have no family. Perfect, just perfect."

Life with the Yavuz family was entirely different from that with the Aydins. Hayriye—Lydia now answered to her Islamic name—was both a domestic and a sex slave. Okan Yavuz was concerned only with keeping Hayriye as his concubine. He delighted in her being sexually available to him at all times. Lydia despised every moment of contact with him. He was, she decided, a truly horrible and evil old man. She was only thirteen. Too young to be his *cariye*, as she heard him boasting. "Hayriye is my cariye," he told his two wives, "and soon she will be my number three—tee hee." His evil laugh convinced Lydia of his malevolence.

It took only a few days for Lydia to learn the dynamics of the household. She understood that Esin, Okan's first wife, was empathetic and would remain kind to her. "I will look after you like you were my daughter," she told Lydia, who, after initial skepticism, came to believe her. Okan's second wife, Yameena, was different.

"Why are you here?" she shouted at Lydia when Okan went out. "He is my husband, and I have born him two fine sons. He needs no more wives. He surely does not need a stupid child like you. A sixty-year-old man! Pshaw. I will make sure he comes to hate you as I do." Lydia was stunned by the hatred and jealousy. But she would not be cowed. "I don't want your old husband," she said, turning her back on Yameena.

* * *

Around five every morning, Yameena would wake Hayriye with a slap to her head. She would pull the covers off her and demand she get up immediately. She would insist that Hayriye help her with her morning wash and dress and then set her to work cleaning the house. Then Hayriye would have to clean out the barns and feed the animals. Most days, Yameena would find some fault with the cleaning and would beat Hayriye with a broomstick. By mid-morning, Yameena would allow Hayriye a piece of bread. Through the afternoons, Hayriye would be given more chores, more criticism, and more physical abuse. Although Esin would sometimes give Hayriye some yogourt, a piece of fruit, or an extra piece of bread, she could not protect her from Yameena's malice.

"You stupid ugly skinny bitch," Yameena would shout at Hayriye, sometimes pulling on her ear or slapping her cheek as she did so, "you can't do anything right can you? You just came here to get my husband. Well, I told you before and I'll tell you again, you are not having him. You could never bear him such sons as I have given him. Soon they will have you instead of him."

The days were horrible, but the nights were much worse. Lydia had seen enough rape while being marched through the desert to know what was happening to her. It was a lot worse than she had imagined. Okan came to her two or three nights a week and his demands hurt her physically and emotionally. Other nights, one of his sons came to her. A few times, both sons came at once and took turns sexually assaulting her. The pain was intense. The shame even worse. For a few weeks, Lydia would spend the time after the men had left her, trying to clean her body and praying for her soul. She got very little sleep.

* * *

As the assaults continued, she learned to mentally disconnect from her body and from what was happening. Now the sexual assault was happening to someone called Hayriye. Not Lydia. Lydia could not feel anything that Hayriye was experiencing. Lydia was happy. She was elsewhere, playing "Ode to Joy" on her violin. It was soothing. That was her reality, not the body on the bed that was being battered and bruised; not the young girl being humiliated. Just Lydia and beautiful music. Hayriye could come back in the morning.

Lydia decided she must leave the Yavuz household when she awoke one morning covered in bruises and hurting more than usual. She ached from the top of her head to her toes. She felt like a wagon had been driven between her legs. She was bleeding from her anus, and it stung intensely when she urinated. She stood, trying to find the strength to leave, when she heard raised voices. She had no difficulty understanding the angry exchange.

"I will not let her go!" shouted Okan.

"But you must," Esin responded tentatively. "You heard what the Pasha said. The Mudros Armistice requires that all Armenian Christian girls who have been kept in Muslim households be returned to their families. We must find Hayriye's family and let her join them."

"I will do no such thing," Okan replied. "She is my cariye and soon she will be my wife. That's it."

"You do not need her," Yameena added. "She is useless. I have to watch her all the time. She does nothing right. I, Yameena, I am your wife. Look at the sons I have given you. You do not need this stupid skinny child."

Okan shouted at the two women. "I have spoken. She will stay and she will become my wife. I will marry her today."

Yameena was not giving up. "You will face severe punishment, husband. She is not worth it. We must get rid of her at once. Never mind finding her family—they are probably dead, anyway. We can just throw her out. I will do it if you don't. She must leave this morning."

"Wife, how dare you speak to me this way? You do not tell me who I shall keep or who I shall marry." Lydia heard the slaps followed by Yameena's loud and angry response. She heard Okan stomp off. There was a moment of silence.

Then she heard Esin sigh loudly. "Come Yameena. We must do what our husband says. Do not anger him further. Come, I will rub some liniment on your face. Hayriye must stay if that is what our husband wants. That poor child."

Esin's comment was the last Lydia heard. She would wait no longer. While the three of them were arguing, she slipped out of the house. It was eerie, but for the first time since her mother had sold her, three-and-one-half years previously, she felt liberated and hopeful. She would, she determined anew, find her mother. In the meantime, she would find someone to help her. She knew there were other farmers in the area. Surely one of them would be kind. Not knowing where she was going, but determined to seek help and get to safety, Lydia said goodbye to Hayriye and ran off across the desert, avoiding the roads.

She ran blindly until she could barely breathe and the pains in her legs forced her to stop. She fell to the ground, panting. She had eaten nothing and had no food with her, and only the clothes she had slept in. She did not know where she was. The only sound, other than her breathing, was from a distant animal. Lydia forced herself to get up. Looking around, she saw a farmhouse in the distance. It was not too far from the Yavuz's farm, but she believed it to be the home of a man she had heard Esin talk about who was known to be kind. Feeling hopeful, she started to run toward it. Lydia did not get too far before her lack of food and water, together with the heat of the sun and her already weakened state, overwhelmed her. Noticing a tree and wanting nothing more than to rest for a moment, she lay down in its shade. She quickly fell into a deep sleep.

Part Two

Aleppo

1918- 1925

11

When Lydia woke, she was lying on a cot, with soft, clean sheets and a blanket over her. She had run away from the Yavuz family and fallen asleep in the desert. Where was she now? She lay still, eyes closed. She heard singing in the distance. She did not understand the words, but knew the voice was not that of a Turk or an Armenian. She opened her eyes, sat up, and looked around.

She was in a dormitory. The room was bare other than two rows of cots and small dressers placed closely together. There were ten cots on each side of the room. The other cots were empty, but each had a neatly folded nightgown placed on a rough fabric cover. There were only two windows. They were small and too high for Lydia to see out of, but she could see that it was daylight outside. At the far end of the room, a light-skinned adult woman was mopping the floor. Lydia realized that this was where the voice was coming from. As she looked, the woman put down her mop and walked toward Lydia, smiling.

Lydia had no idea where she was or who this woman was. She knew only that she had woken up in this cot in this strange room. But she did not feel afraid. The quiet orderliness of the room and the broad smile of the woman coming toward her felt safe. Reaching Lydia, the woman pointed to herself and said, in English, "Jean Clark, American." She held out a hand to Lydia.

Lydia, understanding and pointing to herself, responded, "Lydia Zakarian, Armenian."

Jean led Lydia from the cot down the narrow corridor between the rows of cots to a bathroom at the end of the dormitory. In it were two toilets, two sinks, and one shower. There, Jean helped Lydia out of her clothes and gave her a thorough shower and hair wash. Jean did not comment on the bruises or tattoos on Lydia's body, but her facial expressions made it clear she had noticed them. Lydia felt shame. Her body proclaimed her defilement. The bruises on her buttocks and around her genitals and the tattoos on her face and wrist provided clear evidence. She wondered if she would ever be accepted by anyone. Seeing the sad expression on Lydia's face, Jean wrapped her in a fresh towel, stroked her hair and then gave her a hug. Lydia, sensing she was trustworthy, clung to her. After she towelled her dry, Jean helped Lydia into clean clothes and brushed her hair. Despite being a poor fit, the clothes were nicer than anything Lydia had worn in years.

"Come, child," Jean said, taking Lydia's hand and leading her out of the dormitory across an empty courtyard to another smaller building. While crossing the courtyard, Lydia could hear children singing. It was a welcome sound, but she could not locate it. They went into the smaller building and into an office inside, where Lydia was introduced to a woman sitting behind the desk. The name plate on the desk identified her as an Armenian: Mrs. K. E. Sarkissian. The woman greeted her.

Lydia was thrilled to hear her first language being spoken after so long of hearing only Turkish.

"Where am I?" she asked Mrs. Sarkissian. "Is my mother here? My brother? My dad? How did I get here?

"First, tell me your name, child, and then I will tell you how you came to be with us. Later, we can see if we can find other members of your family."

Speaking quickly, Lydia responded: "I am Lydia Zakarian, my brother is Luke Zakarian, my mother is Mayda Zakarian, and my father is Daron Zakarian. I come from Zeitun. I've lost my family. And I am thirteen years old, or maybe fourteen. I am not sure. First, I had to march over the mountains and through the desert. My Auntie Ruth died, and I had to give away her baby. But I found my mother. But then she sold me like I was a goat and I lived with a family called Aydin. They had nice cows. Then I was sold again and have been living as a slave to a terrible family. So, I ran away. I ran away to the desert. I wanted to find my family. I thought maybe a kind farmer would help me. But I woke up here—what happened? Please tell me. Please."

"Okay Lydia Zakarian, that's a lot! We can talk more about it later. Sit down now and let me tell you how you came to be with us. First," she smiled broadly at Lydia, "I want to say how happy I am to see that you speak and understand Armenian."

"But I am Armenian." Lydia interrupted.

"Yes, but many of the children we bring here have forgotten their Armenian language and speak only the language of the Turks."

"I hate that language." Lydia spoke vehemently. "Please tell me where I am."

"You are in an orphanage, a rescue home, in Aleppo, Syria. It is operated by mostly Americans who came here to help children like you. We are Christians who praise God for giving us this opportunity to serve him. Almost all the children here have been separated from their families. Sadly, they have seen killings, they have been slaves, they have been raped. Is that true for you, Lydia?"

—Tears rolled down Lydia's face. She nodded.

Mrs. Sarkissian continued, "There are around seven hundred children here at the moment, Lydia. The majority are girls. I will tell you more about what you can expect after you have a chance to settle down, but be assured that we will take good care of you. God wills it so. We have a school here, so you will attend classes every day. There are boys in some classes, but boys sleep in separate dormitories and eat in separate dining rooms. The children in your dormitory and classes will be girls around your age."

"First, we need to take you to the nurse here and see if you need any medicines. Many of the children who come here have skin or eye infections, or head lice, and some have diseases you may have heard of— meningitis, typhus, cholera."

"But how did I get here?"

"You were found by a carriage driver. He lived not too far from the Yavuz family from whom you ran. He told us he knew the family well and thought their behaviour brought shame to Islam. It was bad enough, he told us, that the Ottoman government was treating Armenians so cruelly. To see someone in his village do the same was more than he could tolerate. He had seen you several times and guessed what they were doing to you. He had been hoping for a chance to help you and he was outside when he saw you running from the house. You were trying to get away, he believed. He took his carriage to look for you, to make sure you were okay, and to help you. Fortunately, he found you and knew to bring you to us. You were not too far from his house, but you were curled up on the ground, sleeping soundly. He picked you up and drove you here to us without you ever waking up. He is a very good man, Lydia, and we thank God for his kindness."

"You stayed asleep when we put you in your cot and you have slept for over a day. Now, let us get you properly settled in. It is almost time for dinner. You can meet some of the other girls at dinner, and tomorrow you will start your lessons here." Turning to Jean, Mrs. Sarkissian asked her to take Lydia into the dining hall.

"But what about my brother, Luke? Is he here? I need to find him. Please Mrs. Sarkissian..."

"Later Lydia—that's all for now."

12

Jean led Lydia to a dining room with four long tables. Each table had eight chairs and place settings on each side. Not all the places were occupied. Lydia selected a chair at the end of one table as far away from the other children as she could be. The children, who Lydia thought to be between ten and fifteen years old, were not talking. Many of the children—they were all girls, as Mrs. Sarkissian had told her—looked as bewildered as Lydia felt. Some had obvious skin or eye infections. Some had shaved heads. Most were very thin and pale.

Mrs. Sarkissian came in and the girls stood to attention. She led them in a prayer of thanks, recited first in Armenian and then in English. Lydia was thrilled to recognize the prayer as one her family said, but pangs of loneliness accompanied that recognition. As the prayers finished and the girls sat down again, Lydia noticed several of them looking at her. She brought her hands to her face to cover the tattoos. She noted to her shame that no other girl, at least at her table, was tattooed. Lydia felt even more isolated.

Jean Clark brought the food in. After the scavenged seeds from dung, the edible grasses from the desert, the simple food provided by the Aydins and the meagre offerings of the Yavuz family, the pilaf and beans Lydia was given for dinner seemed like a feast for royals. She savoured every mouthful. She enjoyed it so much she temporarily forgot her shame.

After the meal was finished and the plates removed, there was a service. More prayers of thanks were recited, Bible passages were read and hymns were sung. The children recited the prayers and listened to the readings quietly. When the singing started, Lydia was pleased to hear the children sung with enthusiasm. She enjoyed the rare opportunity to express joy that singing provided. The last was a hymn Lydia's father would sometimes sing at sunset: "The Day thou Gavest Lord is Ended." The pangs of loneliness and loss intensified. She could not stop crying as the girls marched from the dining hall to their dormitory's sleeping area, where they quietly and docilely went to bed. Speaking to no one, and ignored by all, Lydia laid down, pulled the cover over her head, and fell into a deep sleep.

A loud bell woke Lydia the next morning. She recalled where she was. Copying the actions of those around her, she dressed quickly and took her turn in the bathroom. The morning started with a prayer meeting in the dining room. Shortly after, the girls were given a breakfast of tea, bread, and a piece of cheese. When breakfast was finished, Lydia was again taken to see Mrs. Sarkissian. Lydia was ready for conversation.

"Where's my brother?" she asked. "Luke Zakarian, did you find him? Is he here?"

"I'm sorry Lydia, but we have no boys by that name here. But I promise you that I will see if any new boys who come here are your brother. We also will try to locate your parents."

Lydia slumped in disappointment.

Mrs. Sarkissian continued. "Now, I want to tell you about what we expect from you and what we offer you while you are living with us."

"You will attend classes every day except Sunday. Sundays are for worshipping God and giving him praise for all we have. Our classes are good. We will make sure you get a sound education that will prepare you for your future. Many of our girls become nurses. You may decide, if you work hard enough, that you want to become a nurse too, or maybe a teacher. Our classes will help you prepare for those occupations. We also require that you attend Bible classes every day. These will help you grow into a good Christian woman. Now, one other thing. Many of our children have to attend Armenian classes because they have forgotten their language. You have done well to remember Armenian, so if you like, we can put you in classes to learn English."

"Yes please, I'd like to learn English and then I can talk to Jean Clark—she has been nice to me. But I also want to learn more music. I play the violin—well, I used to. When the soldiers came, I was practising to play a violin solo at a concert. I even remember what I was going to play—it was Beethoven's "Ode to Joy." Do you know it?" Lydia hummed a few bars.

"That is a wonderful piece. An expression of God's gift to Mr. Beethoven. But we have no violins here, Lydia."

"Oh, well that's okay, I want to learn how to play the oud."

"The only instrument we have here, Lydia, is a piano. We use it in the glory of God, for our services. Perhaps later we can arrange for you to learn to play some hymns on the piano."

Unsure how she felt about that, Lydia stayed silent.

Mrs. Sarkissian continued, "As well as your basic education, we will expect you, like all the children here, to learn skills that help us."

"I don't understand." Lydia interrupted.

"Let me explain. You will learn embroidery and needlepoint and make beautiful linens that we will sell in the villages. Doilies, tablecloths, and pillowcases, for example. The money we raise helps buy your food."

"I don't know how to sew," Lydia said. "What about the boys that are here? What if my brother comes? Will he have to learn to do embroidery? I don't think he'd like that."

"No Lydia. The boys here learn to be tailors, cobblers, or carpenters. And some of the older boys take their goods into town to sell them."

"Can I go into town? Maybe I could find my brother Luke there."

Mrs. Sarkissian did not reply. Rather, she called for an aide to take Lydia to her morning classes.

As with the sleeping and eating arrangements, the classes were segregated by age and sex. Lydia recognized several of the girls from the night before and from breakfast. She was relieved that none were staring at her. While pleased to be ignored, she also thought it would be nice to have a friend to talk to. She wished her school friend Sarah was there.

The morning went by quickly. Her classes were held in Armenian. Discipline was stricter than she had experienced at school in Zeitun. The girls had to maintain good posture while seated at their tables, and undivided attention to the teacher at all times was required. Individual work was to be completed in silence. Lydia had no difficulty with maintaining silence or with the level of work expected. Being in school was a welcome return to being a child rather than a cleaner or a sex slave.

After a lunch of bread and soup, Lydia was called to Mrs. Sarkissian's office. Lydia's hope that her family had been found was quickly dashed.

"Lydia, we have been in touch with our people in Zeitun, and I am sorry to have to tell you that your home and your family's store were destroyed. We have been unable to locate any of your family."

13

Settling into the daily routine of the orphanage, Lydia felt most at peace when she focused on learning during the morning classes. Whether it was English lessons, or mathematics, or Bible studies made no difference. If her mind was occupied with studying, she could, at least temporarily, put aside her loneliness and her shame. She found many of the classes, especially mathematics, easier than they had been at her school in Zeitun, and she took pleasure in excelling.

After being forcibly schooled in the Quran, she delighted in the Bible study classes. They reminded her of the Sunday School classes she had attended with Luke. During one class, the children were asked if they would like to tell the rest of the class their favourite Bible story. Lydia was torn between wanting to talk about Noah and how the ark landed on Mount Ararat, and not wanting to have anyone look at her. She stayed silent. She remained acutely aware and ashamed of the tattoos and what they represented. Several of the children continued to stare at her face. None had been hostile, but neither had any tried to make friends with her.

Since arriving at the orphanage, her body had healed from the deprivations and abuse of the past years. The regular meals and sleep and even the lessons had been curative. But her thoughts continued to plague her. Where was her family? Were they alive? Was her mother even looking for her? Why hadn't her mother kept her promise to come and get her? Did she not want her anymore? Was it possible she knew Lydia was defiled? Was that why she didn't come? Was she ashamed of Lydia? And Luke—was he in an orphanage somewhere else? Was he with their father? Would she ever see any of them again? Would any of them accept her back into the family, given what had happened to her?

She thought also of baby Ani. Would the goatherder and his wife be kind to Ani? Was she growing okay? Such questions, so many questions, swirled endlessly around and around in her mind. There were never any answers. The afternoons were particularly difficult. The activities were less engaging. The swirling multitude of questions seemed louder and more insistent.

Like the other girls at the orphanage, Lydia spent most afternoons learning the art of fancy needlework and handmade lace. Their creations were popular among the market shoppers. They sold well and were an excellent source of income for the maintenance of the orphanage. She understood why Mrs. Sarkissian wanted the girls to produce them. But she did not enjoy the process. She found drawn thread embroidery particularly challenging. Depending on the pattern she was to follow, she would have to pull threads from the fabric she was working on leaving open areas. Sometimes she would have to draw only horizontal threads, and sometimes only vertical ones. The most difficult patterns were those that required both. She would then have to use a finishing stitch, such as a hemstitch around the holes. It was painstaking; she was slow, and the work caused Lydia eye strain. She had difficulty concentrating on the work and keeping the questions that swirled around and around in her brain quiet. She would have much preferred playing her violin. Nonetheless, she did her best to contribute her share of work.

Noting her struggles with embroidery and successes with academics, and realizing she continued to be in a state of emotional turmoil, Mrs. Sarkissian decided she would provide Lydia with the opportunity to learn the piano. She hoped it would be cathartic. Part of her job, she believed, was to help the children heal from their dreadful experiences.

"Lydia," she said, "I know you are having difficulty with the embroidery. I have decided that you may do less sewing and learn to play the piano if you would like to. But Lydia, you will learn to play hymns, and I expect you to play at our services as soon as you are able." Lydia was thrilled.

Playing the piano was more different from playing the violin than Lydia had imagined. But it was easier. She didn't have to worry about tuning the piano without snapping a string, or how to hold it under her chin. She didn't have to think about where to hold the bow or where to place it on the strings. The piano just required hitting the right note, and that seemed more intuitive to Lydia. Where she found the piano more difficult was in needing to read music in the bass clef as well as the treble clef, and in coordinating the chords with her left hand with the melody played by her right hand. Although she had agreed to learn to play hymns, she spent time also playing other music she recalled learning on her violin. She could soon pick out the melody for "Ode to Joy" with her right hand. There were only six notes. Adding the accompaniment with her left hand took a lot of practice. But she practised at every opportunity. Like studying during morning classes, she found playing the piano a therapeutic distraction.

Absorbed in practising hymns one evening, Lydia did not notice that Mrs. Sarkissian had come in and was listening to her. Lydia played through "In the Garden" and then "The Day thou Gavest Lord is Ended." She was surprised to hear applause when she ended.

"Very good Lydia. You will soon be able to accompany our services," Mrs. Sarkissian told her. "You have done very well. Keep practising from that hymnal."

"May I learn something other than hymns, Mrs. Sarkissian?" Lydia asked, relieved that she had not been playing Beethoven.

"Nothing is more important, Lydia. You must always use your skills to spread the gospel and sing his praises. Now, play for me 'Jesus Loves Me.' As your English improves, you will also be able to sing while you play." Lydia obeyed reluctantly. As soon as Mrs. Sarkissian left, she reverted to practising "Ode to Joy."

Lydia kept track of passing time as best she could through the ritual observances of the various church holidays and saint's days. But she was unsure how long she had been at the orphanage. She remained uncomfortable around the other girls and avoided social interaction as much as possible. Everyone seemed kind, but she remained afraid she would be asked about her tattoos and her experiences before arriving at the orphanage. She did not want to talk about either. She was grateful that she was allowed to spend time alone at the piano instead of embroidering linens with the other girls or joining them in courtyard time. She was also grateful for the constant presence of Jean Clark.

Acting as a surrogate mother to the girls in Lydia's dormitory, Jean was affectionate and supportive without being threatening, and without the endless exhortations to give thanks to God that Lydia had come to expect from Mrs. Sarkissian. Jean seemed to sense when Lydia needed a hug and when she wanted to be left alone. She would sometimes sit and brush and braid Lydia's long hair in a soothing manner while talking quietly to her in English. This affection and a growing trust in the relationship together with the piano playing and the morning classes brought Lydia a level of acceptance of her situation beyond that which she had felt at the Aydins. Now, she began to believe in the possibility of a better future. But she remained lonely and ached for her family.

As she learned more English, she formed a more personal relationship with Jean. Lydia was curious about Jean's presence in Aleppo. Jean explained why she had come to Aleppo from America. She had lived in New York where she worked as a nurse, mostly with children. While in New York, she had heard about what the Ottoman Turks were doing to the Armenians—the "starving Armenians," as some called them, she said.

"I read several articles about what was happening that were written by Ambassador Morgenthau."

"I've heard of America and New York, but who is that man?" Lydia asked

"Morgenthau," Jean continued, "was the United States Ambassador to the Ottoman Empire, and he was very upset with what he saw happening to Armenian families. He had friends at a newspaper called the *New York Times* and so he got them to publish articles that he had written about the Armenian situation. He wanted the Americans to know what was going on. I read all those articles, Lydia. They made me feel very sad." She paused for a moment. Lydia could see tears in her eyes. She leaned up against her.

Jean continued, "Morgenthau is a good man, Lydia. As well as writing the articles, he also has worked to raise funds for the survivors, and he has helped get children who were lost in the desert, or had become slaves in Turkish households, like you, to places like this one. I was a member of a Baptist church, and we got involved in what we called the Armenian Relief. Everything I learned led me to decide to come here and do what I could to support children like you."

"But what about your children?" Lydia asked.

"You are my children." Jean replied, giving Lydia a hug.

14

Lydia had been at the orphanage a little more than six months before she gave the daily afternoon piano playing a break. By then she could play every hymn in the hymn book Mrs. Sarkissian had given her. She had taught herself to play "Ode to Joy" properly with both hands. She had no other music. It was getting monotonous, and she was getting lonely.

Her decision to interact with other girls was bolstered by the fact that two weeks earlier, two other children had arrived who had tattoos similar to Lydia's. No one had commented on them. The new girls had not been shunned and had already made friends. As a result, Lydia felt more confident about being among others and thought she might make friends with some girls her age. For the first time, she was interested in joining the exercises and recreation with other children in the courtyard.

When she stepped outside into the bright sunshine, she realized how little time she had spent outdoors over the past few months. Not since the marches through the desert had she spent much time outside. Her chores with the Aydin and the Yuvuz families had been mostly indoors. Since arriving at the orphanage, she had gone into the courtyard for only short periods of time once or twice a week. And only when few others were there, early or late in the day. The glare of the mid-afternoon May sun hurt her eyes, which watered. She moved into a shaded area. She was standing by herself at the edge of the courtyard when she heard a girl's voice that sounded familiar. She was confused. She did not yet know any of the other girls. Then she heard the voice again and realized that it sounded like her best friend from school. Could it possibly be Sarah? It had been so long since they had talked to each other. She peered through her watery eyes. She still could not see clearly, but she heard the voice again, and with her heart beating quickly, she called, "Sarah, Sarah."

"Lydia?" was the questioning reply. "Is that really you, Lydia?" Sarah looked over and immediately recognized her friend. She left the group she was exercising with and ran over to where Lydia stood in a daze. The girls clung to each other, laughing and crying at the same time. Without letting go of each other, they walked to a bench that was at the other end of the courtyard. Sitting close beside each other on the bench, Lydia took Sarah's face in her hands. They were both overcome with emotion.

"What have they done to you? Are you okay? It's been years since I saw you. You look so grown up now. Why haven't I seen you before? Did you just get here?"

With tears running down her face, Sarah answered, "I got here about a week ago, but haven't been outside for more than a few minutes."

"You're so beautiful Sarah. I'm so happy to see you. I can't believe we've found each other. I have longed for you and here you are. It's a miracle. I've been so sad and lost, but I think I will be okay now that you are here."

The girls sat without speaking but holding each other tightly and alternating between giggling and crying. After a few minutes, Lydia asked, "Do you know where your family is? I haven't been able to find Luke or my mother or my father. What if I never see them again, Sarah?"

"Lydia, let me tell you what happened after that Saturday when I was supposed to come over to your place. Then you can tell me where you have been all this time."

Lydia nodded. Sarah sat quietly while a group of younger children ran past them. Then, turning to face Lydia, she took Lydia's hands, held them tightly and began her story.

"I was at home with my parents and my sisters when the soldiers came. They said we had to leave. And they made us leave at once. At the beginning, they forced us to leave Zeitun, but they left us together.

But then, I don't know why, but they took my dad off in a different direction from the rest of us—we never found out where they took him, and we never saw him again. My mum, me, and my sisters then spent months—I don't know how long, but it seemed forever—wandering in the mountains with others who'd also been deported. We passed by villages, we crossed rivers, and we were marched through deserts. It was awful. We never had enough to eat, and we were always exhausted, but we had each other." Sarah stopped and shuddered at the reminiscences. Lydia said nothing. She was flooded with memories she would prefer to forget.

"Anyway," Sarah continued, "after that, everything got worse. I guess we were near some sort of town—I don't know where—when the soldiers made all the girls line up. There was a group of men who they said were looking for girls. They walked up and down the line and picked some of us out. I was one of them. We were just taken from our families and given to those men. The soldiers said we were the lucky ones. They said we had been chosen because we were the best looking. Can you believe it Lydia? We were just kids! It was just awful. I was taken by a Kurd. That was the last time I saw any of my family. I remember my mother and my sisters all crying and holding each other as I was taken away. I was so scared, Lydia."

Lydia, who had sat listening in silence and growing consternation, nodded "I know, Sarah," she said, "I know." Was her friend also raped, Lydia wondered. Should she ask her? What sort of a man was this Kurd? Was he a monster like Okan Yavuz? Could she handle such a conversation? Unsure if she wanted to know, Lydia stayed quiet. Sarah continued her story.

"I was there for a while. I don't know how long. They fed and clothed me, but... I can't talk about that right now, maybe later. So, one day, I was alone when an Armenian man who was a chauffeur came and when he saw me, he said he would help me escape. He took me to the house of a Turkish family he knew."

"Turkish?" Lydia sounded astonished.

"Yes. You would not believe what a good family they were. They had a large house, and they risked their own lives by using the space they had to save Armenians like me. They took me in without question and immediately took me to their room upstairs, where there were seven other Armenian children they were hiding and looking after. It was incredible!" Sarah loosened her grip on Lydia's hands.

"But how did they get away with it? How did they not get caught?" Lydia asked.

"The man—he never told me his real name, we called him Uncle Reuben—with the help of a couple of servants, had found a way to buy food, get it prepared and bring it to us, without any of his wives knowing. Isn't it odd that his servants were more trustworthy than his wives? Anyway, he'd also arranged for his wives to be absent from the house once a week so we could all come downstairs and have a bath. That's how we kept clean." Sarah paused for a moment before continuing, her voice full of emotion.

"There was this little kid, Lydia, she couldn't have been more than three—so cute and so good. But she got sick and even though we all tried everything we could think of, she died. It was awful. But Uncle Reuben even made sure to properly bury her little body—of course he did it in secret or he would have been killed. That's how good he was, Lydia. He was a saint."

"So how did you end up here and when did you come?"

"I stayed at the home of Uncle Reuben until after the Armistice. It must have been about two years, I think. He told us all about the Armistice and he said we could leave if we wanted to. I did not know where to go and I was okay to stay there, so I did for a while. A few of the younger kids stayed too. He was okay with that, but eventually one of his wives found out and insisted we go. He brought all of us—there were four of us, I was the oldest—to this rescue home. He said they would reunite us with our families. I know they're trying, but... you know, I really miss him." Sarah paused for a moment. "Even though it's only been around a week." She sighed. "I've been living in the building across the courtyard. They put me there to keep us together and so that I could help with the younger children. But what about you, Lydia? Did you just get here? "

"I'm in a different building from you, the one that's just for girls aged ten to fifteen, and we have our own dining hall. And it's the first time I've come out during exercise time. I've just wanted to be alone. But not now that I've found you. Let's go and see Mrs. Sarkissian and see if we can live in the same building. We'll be together all the time. Would it be okay if we ask for mine? I know you're supposed to be helping with the younger kids, but maybe someone else can now. I don't want to leave Jean Clark—she treats me well, like a mother, and I have come to love her. You will love her too, Sarah. I am sure. Come! Mrs. Sarkissian, here we come."

"Wait—you didn't tell me about you. What happened to you Lydia? How did you get those blue markings?"

"Not now, Sarah. I can't."

15

Lydia and Sarah both missed their families intensely, but they enjoyed being together and participating in the life of the orphanage. Mrs. Sarkissian had asked them both to help with teaching the younger children. Since moving into Lydia's dormitory, Sarah had missed the children, and Lydia was keen to meet them. She had not given up hope that one day her brother Luke would be among them. They started by helping care for and supervise the preschool children. Over the next two years at the orphanage, they accepted increasing responsibility for the education of the five to eleven-year-olds.

With her reputation of being both smart and hardworking, Lydia was allowed to select her tasks. Her first choice was to teach Bible studies to classes of six to eight-year-olds. Talking to the children about Noah's ark, she often recalled her last conversation with Luke, who at the time had been the same age as the younger children in the class. She also taught mathematics, helped with a girls' choir, and she was teaching a twelve-year-old girl to play the piano. Sarah, who had gained experience looking after the younger children and mastered the English language quickly, was tasked with teaching Armenian and English language classes. She also supervised the daily courtyard exercises.

Now in their mid-teens, Lydia and Sarah also helped with the constant influx of younger children who had been rescued in the desert and brought in for care. There were many. In the course of his employ-ment, a young sheep herder came across many Armenian children in the desert. Some had been abandoned by, and some had run from, the families to whom they had been sold as slaves. The sheep herder took each of the many children he found to the American orphanage. When they were not teaching, Lydia and Sarah helped these new children settle in. They never stopped hoping that among the newcomers they would find their siblings. But they did not recognize any of the hundreds of children they saw over the next few years.

Their responsibilities changed in 1921. Early in the year, Jean Clark had returned to the United States. She had received a letter imploring her to return to help with her ailing mother and her younger sister, who had given birth to twins. Once living in New York, she became involved with the Near East Relief Foundation. It was an American charity, founded in 1915, to assist the Armenian victims of the Ottoman Empire.

The charity had not anticipated the great number of child victims. When Jean joined the group, they were working to increase their capacity to help. Jean had heard about an orphanage that the Foundation had been operating in Syria. Housing well over a thousand children, it was much larger than the one she had worked at where Lydia and Sarah had stayed. Despite its size, it was too small to house the increasing numbers of children who were arriving daily. Opting for the most practical solution, the Foundation reluctantly built a tent camp to accommodate a further eight hundred children. They were now ready to open, but they needed more workers. Jean wrote to Mrs. Sarkissian, asking if she would be okay to let Lydia and Sarah join the staff. Their experience with child refugees, she thought, would be invaluable. Mrs. Sarkissian, appreciating the desperate need for experienced junior teachers at the new facility, agreed. She met with Lydia and Sarah, explained the situation, and asked them if they would go. With some reluctance, they agreed. Although they were hesitant about working for a different charitable organization and a new boss, they were pleased to know their work was valued, and that they could continue to teach and care for Armenian child refugees. They were also pleased to learn that the new camp was close enough that they could keep in touch with Mrs. Sarkissian in case their siblings showed up.

Lydia and Sarah moved into the camp as soon as it opened. Once there, they had no time to consider whether their decision had been the right one. They were endlessly busy looking after the many children who arrived on a daily, sometimes hourly, basis. They also continued teaching. In the mornings, Sarah held Armenian language classes for the many children who had been forbidden to speak it, and therefore forgotten it. Lydia taught math and Bible studies as before. In the early afternoons, they both supervised recreation and organized sports. There was no opportunity at the tent camp for Lydia to continue with her music. Reluctantly, she filled her spare time doing the needlework that she had disliked and previously avoided as much as possible.

As at other orphanages caring for Armenian refugee children, sales of fine linens and lace were a key means of funding. Lydia and Sarah were compelled to contribute. Lydia had long stopped trying to perfect the pulled and drawn thread work and so she concentrated on hand made lace. As her work improved, she found the repetitive motions soothing and gained satisfaction from the finished pieces. She was proud of her lace collars, doilies, and table runners, and they sold well. The busy schedule kept her exhausted. That helped her sleep.

In the new environment, Lydia's self-consciousness about her tattooed face was lessened. One reason was she had learned to accept that her fears of being ostracized or ridiculed because of the tattoos were unfounded. Most ignored them. The second reason, one that both comforted and saddened her, was that she had noticed an increasing number of girls in the camp arriving with very similar markings. One of the younger girls, whose tattoos were similar to Lydia's, had asked her about them.

"Do you mind having those marks on your face?" she had asked Lydia. "Do the others tease you about it? Can get rid of them? I hate them." She finished with a sigh.

"I understand. I don't like them at all, and I don't know of anyway to get rid of them. But, you know, other people don't say anything, so I've found it best to pretend they don't exist. Most of the children here

have been hurt in some way. I hope you will make friends like I have."
Lydia gave the girl a hug.

Lydia no longer thought about the tattoos frequently. Nonetheless, she maintained her belief that she would never marry. She would never have her own family because no one could possibly want her with such obvious defilement. Instead, she would stay at the camp, where she felt safe and accepted there. She would devote her life, in the service of God, to helping as many others as she could.

Then a letter arrived from Jean. It evoked memories that Lydia had tried to repress. The envelope was addressed to Lydia. She opened it and read the letter aloud to Sarah.

February 20, 1922

My dear Lydia and Sarah,

I hope this letter finds you both well and happy at the camp. I can't tell you how pleased I am that you agreed to go there. I miss you both very much and hope one day to see you again. I am sure you are both helping many children. I heard that there are still many children who are coming to the camp, still so many without their families, so many that are hurting. It makes me very sad. I miss being there with you.

I am generally fine, although it does feel strange being back in New York. My mother is recovering, and my sister is coping, although I do spend a lot of time helping her with the babies. They're very cute—you'd love them. She calls them Elizabeth and Edward—such big names for such little people!

Anyway, I am writing because I have news that I think you will be interested in. I have just learned that on March 15 of 1921, an Armenian student murdered Talat Pasha in Berlin. Can you believe it! How did we not know this before???? As you probably know, this is the man that most people hold responsible for the deportation and killing of so many of your people. Possibly even your family members. I assume you still have not found any of them. Apparently, TP resigned from the Union and Progress Party right after the war ended in 1918 and went to Berlin from Istanbul.

The student (sorry I can't remember his name) is said to have gone to Berlin intending to kill Talat Pasha. Apparently, he eventually tracked him down and followed him as he walked down a street or left his house or something like that. The news report said that the student shot TP at close range—right in the head and that he died instantly! Now we, as Christians, don't want to condone murder even of such a corrupt man, although I can't help but think it is a fitting end for a tyrant. But anyway, you might not want to rejoice too much over his death. (But it's okay if you do!).

Here's more news that I think you'll be pleased to hear. The student was charged with murder. A trial was held in June of last year. He readily admitted to having killed TP. I recall that it alleged in the report that he said, "I have killed a man but I am not a murderer." Interesting concept, don't you think? Well, the jury agreed with him, and their verdict was not guilty. I confess I gasped when I read that. Turns out that his lawyer argued fervently that TP was indeed chiefly responsible for the massacre of many thousands of Armenians—that the real murderer was TP and not the student. I guess the jury agreed. I don't know if he left any children. I think it said that he was forty-seven years old, so probably he did, but he did leave a wife—her name is Hayriye.

Lydia stopped reading. Her face turned ashen, her hand shook, and her eyes filled with tears as she was flooded with the memories that she had tried so hard to block.

"What's wrong?" Sarah was stunned by Lydia's sudden change of demeanour.

Lydia passed the letter to Sarah. "Here," she said, and ran.

16

Sarah ran after her friend. She caught up with her at their tent where Lydia was lying on her cot in a fetal position, sobbing. Sarah sat beside her and silently stroked Lydia's back until her sobs subsided.

"Lydia? Wasn't that good news about Talat Pasha? Why are you so upset?" Sarah asked.

Controlling her sobs as best she could, Lydia answered, "Yes, yes, I am glad that he is dead. It's not that I'm upset about it, it's hearing that name, Hay… Hay" She could not continue.

"Tell me Lydia, why is a name upsetting you so much? Do you know someone called Hayriye? I don't remember anyone by that name in Zeitun. You've never told me what happened to you before you we met up at the orphanage. Did someone called Hayriye hurt you on your journey? What happened to you? Tell me Lydia. You know I'd never judge you, and you might feel better if you share your troubles with me." She put her arm around Lydia's shoulders. "Come on Lydia, talk."

Lydia shuddered. "I'll try. I have prayed and prayed that I would forget, but seeing that name…."

"Let's go for a walk and maybe you can talk while we are walking."

"I'll try." Lydia responded as she sat up and wiped her eyes.

"That last Saturday at home in Zeitun, you know the one where you were going to come over, well I went to the river to help my Aunt Ruth with her laundry. We had hardly started when soldiers came and made us leave everything and they forced us into a crowd of people who were being forced to march out of Zeitun. For many weeks, we marched across the desert. We were scared, tired, and hungry."

"Wasn't your aunt expecting a baby?" Sarah asked.

"Oh Sarah, I tried to save her. I tried to save the baby. Baby Ani." Lydia's sobs prevented talking. They sat in silence for several minutes. Sarah kept her arm tightly around Lydia. "It's okay, Lydia, you don't have to tell me now."

"I need to," Lydia said, a few moments later. She did not provide details of Ruth's death or what happened with her baby, but described finally finding her mother, her anger at being sold, and her life with the Aydins.

"Sounds like you really liked the cows." Sarah smiled. "But who was Hayriye?"

Lydia took a deep breath. "Me," she said. She explained the Aydin's insistence that she become Muslim and their use of a Muslim name for her.

"Was it so bad?"

"Not at first. But they sold me to an evil man who defiled me. He hurt me and his sons hurt me, but I kept telling myself it was Hayriye, not me. Then I got away, Sarah. I ran, and now I found you."

"You are the bravest person I ever met, Lydia," Sarah said, realizing that she should not probe further. "And the kindest. You've done nothing but help other children since we found each other. I'm so proud to be your friend."

Talking about her experiences remained difficult for Lydia. But it had also been cathartic and, with the support of her friend, had lessened the gnawing feeling of impending danger that she usually felt. She wondered if she would ever be able to fully divulge the sexual abuse that she had experienced.

She turned the conversation to their present circumstances, and the children for whom they were caring and teaching.

"What do you want next?" Sarah asked Lydia. "I want to marry and have lots of children. Do you? Of course, I want my children to grow up in a regular home—not a camp like this one."

"I'll never marry." Lydia was emphatic. "Look at me, Sarah—no man will want me. There is no way I can get rid of these tattoos or change what they represent. And I don't think I could be with a man—you know what I mean. I couldn't bear it. I like being with these children here—they have no one, and they need so much love. I'm happy to be here teaching the children and helping them grow into good Christians. I'm pretty sure it's God's will that I stay here and look after the children."

Lydia did sometimes wonder if God had a different plan for her. She still missed her family, and she missed playing the piano. But she knew she should be grateful to God for keeping her safe. Increasingly, she turned to reading the Bible and singing hymns. She continued to delight in teaching the children Bible stories. She would often ask them the question she remembered was the last one she asked Luke: Which animals would you take on the ark? None had ever answered like her brother. She often reflected on how happy she and Luke had been before that awful day when the soldiers came. She tried to imagine the joyful and inquisitive Luke she remembered as a teenager, hoping he was somewhere safe.

"I don't know about God's plan, Lydia, but I don't think you will be staying here." Sarah responded. "There are fewer children coming all the time. Some will soon be old enough to move on, and I heard rumours that the camp may run out of funding. What will you do if or when the camp closes?"

* * *

Nineteen twenty-three came and the waves of incoming refugee children subsided. With fewer children arriving, Sarah was restless, and Lydia suspected Sarah was looking for a way to leave the camp. Lydia noticed Sarah was interested in a man who made deliveries to the camp twice weekly. He always took the time to chat with the children. Sarah made a point of being around at delivery time, and they quickly struck a friendship. Lydia teased Sarah about how she seemed to glow after her chats with him. It was no surprise to Lydia when Sarah told her that she had met the man she wanted to marry.

The marriage took place less than a year later, in May of 1924. It was not a traditional wedding. The marriage was not arranged, and the bride had no family and no home. The groom's family was of modest means. There was no money for the typically lavish food, and too few connections for the characteristic large number of guests at an Armenian wedding. Nonetheless, Sarah met and was approved by Paul's parents, and they arranged a small wedding with most of the attendees on Sarah's side being staff from the camp. Sarah moved into a house in Aleppo with her husband, Paul Maradonian. She promised to write to Lydia at least once a week and to visit as often as she could.

Sarah's letters to Lydia indicated her friend had found the life she wanted. She was content looking after her home and her husband and looking forward to having children of her own. Lydia was pleased for Sarah, but her resolve to stay at the camp with the children was not lessened.

* * *

One afternoon, Mrs. Sarkissian came for a visit. Lydia was delighted to see Mrs. Sarkissian. She had not realized that she had missed her. They embraced, and Lydia showed Mrs. Sarkissian around the camp. They discussed the state of the children who were there. Mrs. Sarkissian then asked about Sarah and was pleased to hear that she was happily married to a good Armenian man and living in Aleppo.

"Come, let us have some tea Lydia" she said. "I have received a letter that I want to share with you. I think it may be good news for you."

Reaching into the bag she was carrying, Mrs. Sarkissian pulled out an envelope with a stamp on it that Lydia didn't recognize. She peered at it and thought it seemed like it was from England. Could it have something to do with her parents or with Luke? She was hopeful. Mrs. Sarkissian opened the envelope and pulled out several thin handwritten pages and a photograph.

17

Mrs. Sarkissian told Lydia that the writer of the letter was a Mr. Dikran Vartounian, who was currently living in England. He had written to Mrs. Sarkissian in search of a bride. He had enclosed a small photograph of himself that she showed Lydia.

"See what a nice-looking Armenian man he is, Lydia. He has such gentle big eyes, and such lovely curly dark hair. This is such a wonderful opportunity for you to have your own home and family," she told an alarmed Lydia. "Of all the young women who have worked with me, I do believe you are the most suitable for this man. That is why I have come here today."

"Please, no!" Lydia managed to say.

"Wait, Lydia. Let me read you the letter and you will see why I think you should be his bride. Or maybe I will just tell you about this man—who he is—and then we can read the letter."

"Mr. Vartounian, like you Lydia, was a child in Armenia when the Ottoman rulers attacked the Armenians. He was a little older than you were—he was twelve, I believe you were ten. He lived with his family in Van. Many of the Armenians in Van had barricaded themselves in the city's Armenian neighbourhood, but his family stayed where they were in their home on Lake Van. On one dreadful day in April of 1915, Mr. Vartounian, Dikran, saw his father, who was a schoolteacher, and another man, go to help an Armenian woman who was being harassed by some Ottoman soldiers. The soldiers shot and killed both men. That day, Dikran, his mother, and his three-year-old brother Davit left Van and headed off toward Yerevan."

"Oh!" Lydia's eyes widened, and she paid more attention. Mrs. Sarkissian continued.

"Yes, you can imagine how he must have been feeling. They had a long and difficult journey. Sadly, Davit did not make it. Dikran said that Davit could not keep up with the trek across the mountain passes, so his mother carried him. As she grew weaker and more exhausted, he carried Davit. There was never enough food or water and just as they approached Yerevan, little Davit died in Dikran's arms—presumably of starvation."

"No," sobbed Lydia, the tears running down her face as she was reminded of Ruth's death and parting with baby Ani.

Mrs. Sarkissian continued. "Distraught over losing her younger son, Dikran's mother could not adapt to life in Yerevan. Her restlessness drove her to move again. This time, they went south to Baghdad. But she still felt unsettled. They stayed in Baghdad for less than a year before leaving for Scotland, where they settled in Glasgow."

"Scotland? Why?" Lydia was incredulous.

"He didn't say, but it might simply have been that since they could not return home, they moved to wherever felt safe. Perhaps they did not feel safe in Baghdad. Or maybe that was where they could go as immigrants. I don't know. But I think it likely that his mother was so upset losing her husband and her son that she just needed somewhere to start over that was very different. And you know, Lydia, sometimes when people cannot rid themselves of inner pain, they keep changing their external circumstances. Of course, it rarely helps much. Anyway, back to Dikran. He seems to have done well in Scotland. He says that he improved his English skills, finished high school, and then he trained to be a missionary. You see what a good man he is, Lydia."

"So, is he a missionary now?"

"No. He wrote that just as he was finishing his training, his mother died, and he went through a very challenging time. For a while, he questioned his faith and God's goodness. And like his mother, he needed to physically move to cope with the sadness and loss. He settled on London, in England, where he is now. He plans to work there for a few more years—he is working in a bakery—he will then go back to his goal of becoming a missionary. Dikran is still a young man, Lydia, only twenty-four. There are many years left for him to do God's service."

"But what does this have to do with me?" Lydia asked.

"Well," Mrs. Sarkissian smiled at Lydia, "like so many others, he has suffered tremendously from losing all his family, so now he wants more than anything to get married and have a family of his own. He believes having a family will allow him to move beyond the memories that torment him. He wants an Armenian wife. A wife who will understand, who shares his belief in God and the importance of family. I think that would be you, Lydia."

"But I am happy here and I don't want to be with any man."

"Lydia, I have heard from my colleagues here that this camp may not exist much longer. I have spoken with them about you and this offer. We are in agreement that you should accept Mr. Vartounian. Where are you going to go? Unfortunately, I don't have space for you to return to our orphanage. You must consider how you are going to live. Marriage provides the opportunity for you to have a stable and secure life."

"But even if that's what I wanted, I have all these tattoos which I cannot get rid of. This man will not want a woman who has been defiled and whose face tells the world what she has done."

"Lydia, listen to the next part of his letter. After he talks about his past, he writes:"

I know that many of the Armenian girls that were taken during the marches are tattooed and are ashamed of the way they look because of that. I do not mind. In fact, I would be honoured to help such a young woman with overcoming her past, just as I hope being part of a family will help me overcome my suffering. Looks of any kind do not concern me. I want a good Christian woman who is healthy, who will be a good and faithful wife. One who is willing to bear me children, one who cares about God, not riches. If you know of such a young woman, I will pay for her journey to England. I will protect and cherish her always. Together we will have hope for a better future, together we will overcome the pain of our past.

"Lydia, I will come back tomorrow, and we will talk some more. I realize this is a surprise and you need some time to think about it, and to pray for guidance in your decision."

Throughout the rest of the day, Lydia experienced a range of emotions. She tried to understand why Mrs. Sarkissian had selected her and why she thought it was such a wonderful opportunity. She thought about Dikran Vartounian and how he sounded like a nice man, but a man nonetheless. Could she ever feel comfortable in the presence of a man, let alone engage in the sexual activity that would be essential for having children?

She thought also about how nice it might be to raise her own children—to watch them grow, to teach them about Noah's ark and the love of Jesus, to teach them to play the piano. But how could she go to England? How would she get there? How could she live in yet another country—one she knew nothing about? If she left Syria, it would be to return to Armenia, not to go to the other side of the world. What if her mother or her brother were still looking for her? How would they ever find her in England? That night, she prayed for a sign to help her. She did not sleep well.

18

A letter from Sarah arrived two hours after Lydia had struggled through breakfast the next morning. Sarah had written to tell Lydia that she and Paul were leaving Aleppo to move to Constantinople. Sarah would, she wrote, no longer be able to visit Lydia at the camp. She had also heard more rumours that the camp might shut down. But she promised to write regularly. They must always write to each other, she said, no matter where they lived.

Lydia's first thought was how much she would miss knowing that her closest friend was nearby. Her second thought was that this may be the sign from God that she had prayed for. Perhaps she should agree to the marriage. The thought was disturbing. It would entail moving to a strange country to live with a stranger. A man. A man who would touch her in ways she did not want to be touched. She replied to Sarah, explaining her current dilemma.

For the next hour, Lydia was distracted by teaching Bible study classes to the children. She relaxed as the children enthusiastically sang "Jesus Loves Me" while she accompanied them on the piano—a recent and welcome addition to the camp. But the relaxation was short-lived. After a modest lunch of fresh bread and yogourt with fruit, she received word from Mrs. Sarkissian that both the tent camp and the original camp she had lived at would close within a year, as soon as they could find homes for the remaining children. Mrs. Sarkissian was going to America. Lydia would have to find somewhere else to live and some other position.

Lydia decided it must be God's plan for her to go to England. She saw no other options. Rather than feeling pleased, she felt hollow inside.

She knew she would have to leave the safety and stability of life in the camp. She would have to leave the children, many of whom she loved as though they were her own. Anticipating all the changes that would occur in her life was terrifying.

What terrified her the most was the expectation that once he saw her tattooed face, Dikran would have nothing to do with her. Surely, she thought, he could not expect how shameful it is. What would she do in a strange country, rejected and on her own? Throughout the afternoon lessons and evening prayer service, Lydia fretted. Once she went to bed that night, she devised a plan. She would ask Mrs. Sarkissian to send this Dikran man a photo of her face. If he still wanted her, she would go. Hoping and expecting that he wouldn't, she fell asleep.

The next day, she was able to send a message to Mrs. Sarkissian. Two days later, Mrs. Sarkissian took Lydia to a photo studio. Lydia had never had her photo taken and was nervous about the whole procedure. She stood stiffly when asked to pose, one hand resting on the table that she stood beside.

"You must focus the picture on my face," Lydia instructed the photographer. He nodded without comment. "I need to be sure that he sees how awful I really look," she said to Mrs. Sarkissian. "He needs to see that these tattoos have not faded, but continue to tell everyone who sees me that I am defiled."

"I understand, child. You hope that he will not want you once he sees your face. Am I right?"

Lydia sighed. The photo was taken.

"Do you want to write him a letter also?" asked Mrs. Sarkissian.

"I wouldn't know what to say. Can you do it for me, please?"

Lydia could not remember feeling as stressed as she felt waiting for a response since she had arrived in Aleppo over six years ago. She wrote a letter to Sarah explaining the situation and asking for her thoughts on what she should do. She impatiently waited for Sarah's response.

Adding to her anxiety were the ongoing efforts to find homes for all the children before the camp closed. Each day, a few more of the children Lydia loved were gone. She was happy for them but missed them intensely. The reality of limited time at the camp was increasingly hard to ignore. Her classes were shrinking in size, as many of the younger children she so enjoyed teaching and spending time with had gone to live with families in the area. She was growing more fearful of her future. How much longer could she stay while all others were leaving?

When Mrs. Sarkissian came to Lydia's room with Dikran's response, she had a broad smile on her face.

"He sounds so poetic, Lydia," she said. "Listen to this." She read from the letter.

> March 14, 1925
>
> My dear Mrs. Sarkissian,
>
> Thank you for the letter and sending the photo. I do under-stand Lydia's concern, but she has no need of it. Lydia's inner beauty shines through and there is no tattoo on earth that could hide it. Her beautiful eyes reveal a soul that is full of love and God's grace. But they also reflect a great deal of pain. I hope and plan to help her overcome that. I have always believed that "amor vincent omnia."

Here Mrs. Sarkissian paused and chuckled at the expression on Lydia's face. "Shall I read on?"

Lydia nodded.

> As I wrote in my earlier letter to you, I have no concern with the tattoos. To me, they mean only that she is a brave young woman who has suffered and must now be loved. And I promise to love, cherish, and protect Lydia always if she is so kind as to come and be my wife. I will make her happy! Together we will put our sad histories aside, we will live each day to the glory of God, and we will raise our children in a loving Christian

Armenian family. My dear Mrs. Sarkissian, please let Lydia know that I love her already and I cannot wait to meet her and make her my wife.

"I will leave this letter with you, child, and I will come back in two days for your answer." Mrs. Sarkissian laid the letter on Lydia's bed, gave her a brief hug, and left. Lydia sat stunned. The response had not been at all what she had been expecting and hoping for. She felt more confused than ever. Beautiful? Love? Her? What sort of man was this Dikran?

Sarah's letter came the next day. Sarah encouraged Lydia to accept the offer of marriage and a fresh start. She expressed her astonishment that Lydia would hesitate to accept such a generous opportunity to put the past behind and move on. Sarah stressed how satisfying life was with a loving husband to cook for, and your own home to care for. She wrote about how joyous it felt to know you could raise children of your own. Sarah ended with noting the reality that the chances of Lydia seeing her mother or brother again were slim to none. "Go to him. Move on with your life."

Part Three

Aleppo to London

1925 –1945

19

Twenty-one-year-old Lydia stood on the dock staring with a mix of amazement and horror at the ship that was about to take her to a new life. She was shivering from fear and the weather. It was an unusually cold and windy day. She stood with her left hand holding her hat and her right hand clutching her bag. The ocean looked menacing and endless, the ship too small and battered to stay afloat. She was hesitant to go further but found herself swept along with the noisy crowd who were embarking. Along with the many other emigrants, Lydia walked toward and then up the gangplank.

Once aboard the Lucretania, she realized her fears were well-founded. It was indeed a ancient ship. A gruff and unsavoury looking steward led her and other third-class passengers through narrow and steep passageways and down ladders until they arrived at a large room at the bottom of the ship. It was far from the cabin she had envisaged travelling in. The ceiling height was around six feet, and there were no portholes. There were already several women and a few children sitting on the double-deck bunks that lined the walls. The row of bunks in the middle remained empty. Realizing that the middle of the ship should feel more stable, Lydia sat on the straw mattress on the bunk at one end of the middle row. There was just enough space for her to sit up without banging her head on the upper bunk. She looked around with growing apprehension for sanitary conveniences. There were a few wash basins and toilets behind a partition in one corner of the room. It was difficult for her to understand how these would be sufficient if the room filled.

She fought the panic that threatened to overcome her. She wondered if and how she would survive the trip to Marseille.

More and more women continued to arrive. They appeared to be of all ages, including, she noted, several children and babies. With a growing sense of anguish, she watched as rats and roaches scurried out of their way. Soon the bunks were all taken, yet still more women and girls arrived. Sharing bunks became a necessity. Lydia noticed that although many languages were being spoken, the women shared a look of despair and disbelief. Was it possible, she wondered, that these conditions would become as intolerable as those she'd experienced on the march from Zeitun, or at the refugee camp? At least there were no soldiers, she told herself. She wondered if any of the women around her had experienced the marches, the hunger, the rapes; they had prepared her well to cope with whatever hardships the journey would bring. Was this what all ships were like? Had Dikran known of this?

The roar of the engines, the shriek of the ship's whistle, and the sudden jolt of movement brought Lydia from her reverie. They were leaving. She, Lydia Zakarian, really was on this ship and God willing she would get safely to England. Beyond that, she could not imagine. She remained sitting on the bunk, clutching her bag close to her chest. In it were her total possessions—a change of clothing and several pieces of her lace work that Mrs. Sarkissian had kept for her. They brought her little comfort. They had only just started the journey and already the room was hot, noisy, and stank of oily fumes.

Lydia noticed the girl immediately. She was among the last to arrive. She looked young and terrified and was obviously pregnant. The tattoos on her face mirrored those of Lydia's. Their eyes met in mutual recognition. She looked at Lydia questioningly and Lydia, understanding, nodded. She moved over to one side of the mattress to make way for the girl.

"Thank you. My name is Yasmine." Lydia was overjoyed to hear her native Armenian tongue.

"Are you going to be all right?" Lydia asked, looking at Yasmine's abdomen.

Understanding what she was really asking, Yasmine explained.

"I think so. I should be fine as long as we get to Marseille on time. My future husband is meeting me there."

"But," said Lydia, "you are with child."

"Mr. Hakob Gabrelian, the man who will be my husband, is a widower with three children: two girls, aged five and seven, and a three-year-old boy. He wrote a letter to the orphanage where I was living," said Yasmine. "He wanted an Armenian bride and said that he would welcome one who had a child."

"That's hard to believe," Lydia said.

"Well," Yasmine continued, "in 1916, he lost his parents to the Turks and his sister was taken by a Kurdish family who abused her terribly. He wrote that she had been forced to marry and bear one of them children. After giving birth to a second child, she died. He seems to feel that if he cares for someone like me, then he will atone for what happened."

"What do you mean, someone like you?" Lydia asked.

"I too lost my parents and was forced to marry a Kurd. But I escaped before I knew I was pregnant and got to the orphanage where I was living. This man, Mr. Gabrelian, is giving me and this child a chance to live a decent life. And I will cherish him and care for the children he has now. I am very tired." She lay down, closed her eyes and was soon asleep.

The next two weeks were hard. Lydia took comfort from the strength and resilience of her new friend, but the rough seas, lack of ventilation, and poor sanitary conditions created insufferable conditions. There were some similarities to the conditions at the camps, but at least on the ship there was cooperation among the women, and there was no violence. By the end of the third day, seasickness was rampant among the crowded hot third-class cabin, and many were suffering from skin infections caused by scratched flea or rat bites. The food they were provided was sufficient for survival, but it was bland, repetitive, and never enough. More and more passengers became sick. Lydia noted that at least three women and two children had died since the journey started. She did not know how much longer it would take to reach Marseille. She was not sure she would make it.

Early in the morning of the second to last day at sea, Lydia woke to see her friend writhing on the mattress, holding her abdominal area. Please God, no, not here, not now, she thought.

"Help me, Lydia," Yasmine whispered as she rolled around. "It's coming too soon. I am so scared, oh the pain—it's awful. Something's wrong Lydia, please help me."

Lydia looked around. Most were still asleep. She was flooded with memories of the awful night in the desert with her Aunt Ruth and the birth of baby Ani. She could feel herself panicking. Lydia prayed for guidance and strength, and the health of the mother and child. This time, her prayers were answered.

Four hours after being awoken, Lydia was cradling a new passenger, a little girl whose birth had been remarkably quiet and easy. Yasmine had been able to nurse her new infant and was now sleeping comfortably. Using her nightgown, Lydia had cleaned her friend and the bed and disposed of the placenta before most of the other passengers were awake. Lydia wrapped the baby in Yasmine's coat. Looking at the newborn, Lydia felt a peace she had not felt since she had been at home with her family, since she had been a young girl practising her violin while her mother cooked cabbage dolmas.

"What name will you give this beautiful baby?" she asked when Yasmine woke up and took the baby to her breast.

"What else but your name?" she answered with a smile. "This little miracle is Lydia."

20

Disembarking at the Port of Marseille, Lydia had just enough time to meet Hakob Gabrelian and say goodbye to Yasmine and baby Lydia before boarding the overnight train to Calais. Despite the discomfort of sitting all night, she felt more relaxed being on land and managed to get some sleep.

The last leg of her journey was sailing across the English Channel on the Saxon. She did not have a cabin booked since Dikran had explained that the trip took less than a day. She would travel in a common area for second-class passengers. After her experience in steerage on the Lucretania, she was untroubled by that. But she would not have access to what she really wanted and desperately needed—a thorough wash, clean clothing, and a comfortable bed. That, she knew, would have to wait.

As she found her sitting area, Lydia realized that her intense fears had been replaced by curiosity and a sense of competence to deal with whatever awaited her. It had felt good to have delivered the baby, her namesake. With God's help, she had more than simply survived the trip. She was even able to ignore the stares at her face from some of the other passengers. But she still had concerns. What would she do if Dikran was not at the port to meet her when she arrived? Or perhaps even worse was the question of what if he was there, but he was far different from what he had described, or what if she hated him on sight? Or what if he took one look at her with her dirty clothing and scraggly dirty long hair and walked away? Stop, she told herself. What if it all works out well?

She did her best to tidy up before disembarking. Finding a toilet and washbasin, she washed her face, and after running her wet hands through her long hair, she put her hair into two long thick braids. She could do nothing about her dress.

Her first sight of London filled her with dismay. It was flat, damp, foggy, and grey. When she disembarked, the docks were chaotic, busy, and noisy. The customs and border control line was long. Lydia presented proof of her impending marriage and the agent waved her forward. She waited in the large and crowded hall, and was almost considering turning around and getting back on the ship when she caught sight of Dikran. She recognized his face immediately from the photograph she had received. He had a red carnation in the lapel of his coat as he had said he would and was waiting exactly where he had described he would be, just outside the customs hall. He would have to be patient, she thought, as she joined the long line for entry to London.

Forty minutes later, she emerged. Dikran was in the same spot. She thought he looked anxious. Feeling obliged to go through with her promise, particularly given the uncertainty of alternatives, she walked toward him nervously. His face lit up with a broad smile when he saw her. She froze. She was simultaneously relieved to see that he was there and annoyed that she had lost the best excuse possible for returning to the ship and going back to Marseille.

Travelling into the city by train, Lydia was pleased that Dikran verbally welcomed her and then sat quietly beside her. Rather than embracing or touching her as she had feared he might, or asking her questions, he seemed to be aware that she was tired and nervous. She was grateful. He had informed Lydia in an earlier letter that she would stay in a boarding house until the wedding. She was eager to get there and rest. During the short walk there from the train station, Dikran told her about the area and explained that the boarding house was just a ten-minute walk from his flat. Upon arrival, Lydia was greeted at the door by the owner, Mrs. Wood. Handing over her bag, which he had been carrying, Dikran wished her a good rest and said he would come by the following morning.

Lydia was reassured to find that she had her own small, portioned area of a room in the boarding house. It was clean and furnished with a single bed, a small wardrobe, a wooden chair, and a washbasin. There was a shared toilet in the hallway. To Lydia, this was luxury accommodation. After she unpacked her few belongings, she went to the common sitting area. Mrs. Wood met her there. Lydia was thrilled to see the sitting area contained a piano. She asked Mrs. Wood if she would be allowed to play it.

"Yes, dear," Mrs. Wood replied, "but only between ten in the morning and seven in the evening." She continued to inform Lydia of the other house rules.

She then showed Lydia the communal dining room and explained that Dikran had paid not only for three weeks lodging but also for full board. Lydia was happy to hear this. Feeling more relaxed than she had for a long time, Lydia returned to her room, removed her dress, lay on the bed, and immediately fell asleep. She slept through the rest of the day and all through the night.

In the morning, she felt rested for the first time in as long as she could remember. She was also very hungry. She had a quick wash as soon as there was space in the bathroom, got dressed, and, appreciating the aroma of toast, went to the dining room. The long tables were close together and one appeared dangerously close to the fireplace, where embers of coal glowed. Lydia was glad to see that a fire had been lit; it was a chilly day for September. She looked around and found an empty seat. The girl beside her smiled.

"Hello," she said, "you must be new here? Do you speak English? Are you Jewish? You sorta look Jewish."

"No," Lydia replied in perfect English but with a notable accent, "I'm not Jewish. My name is Lydia Zakarian and I'm Armenian."

"Yea? Well, my name is Gladys Smith and I'm a Brit. You know you're not the only one who's Armenian. See that girl there coming outta the kitchen—she's Armenian. There's folks here from all over. If you listen, you'll hear lotsa different languages because a lot of the women here are refugees. I'm not. I just came to London recently from Middlesex and am just staying here 'til I get my own home."

Lydia bit into her toast and had a sip of tea. "It seems nice here." she commented.

"Yes. Well, it's okay for meeting other women, but there's so many bloody rules. Worst is there's a strict curfew of nine-thirty and we're not allowed to have any boys or men visit. I hate that. It's hard for me to spend time with my boyfriend."

Lydia did not reply but was quietly happy to hear that men were not allowed.

After breakfast, Lydia saw the girl Gladys had mentioned was Armenian. She was taking dishes to the kitchen. Lydia went up to the girl and introduced herself in Armenian. She immediately put the dishes down and hugged Lydia. After a quick introduction, Lydia asked her new friend Eva questions about the boarding house and London. She also wanted to know Eva's history—why and how she was there. Lydia went to the kitchen with Eva to help with washing the dishes. They talked as they cleaned up.

"After my parents were killed, I spent almost ten years in an orphanage in Yerevan," Eva explained. "I was more than ready to leave when I was told I should come to England to marry this man. He had sent a letter to my orphanage asking for a bride. I still don't know why they picked me. But anyway, in his letter, he said he was aged twenty-five, and that he was a banker with lots of money and a big house. Sounded pretty good—not that I care that much about money, but it would have been nice to be with a successful man and have a nice home. So, I agreed and came over. That was about three months ago now."

"Then why are you here?" Lydia asked, as Eva paused her tale while she put a pile of plates in the cupboard.

"Because," Eva said, "it was all a lie. When I met him, I realized right away that he was neither twenty-five nor rich. I learned quite soon that he was forty-eight. I'm twenty-one. And as for being rich, no way. It turned out that he shared a small house with a friend. Oh, and of course he was not a banker, he was a street sweeper. Like I said, it's not that I wanted money, but I certainly did not come all this way to marry a fraud, a liar."

"I'm so sorry," Lydia replied, now wondering about Dikran. "Are you okay?"

"Well, for now, I am living here and working in the kitchen to pay my way. I am hoping to get a job with the Lord Mayor's Fund. I'm not sure if they are still operating or how much longer they will, but I know they were funding some wonderful work in Yerevan—they were running an orphanage, a feeding station, and a shelter for homeless children. I would love to help with that. What about you?'

"My story is similar to yours. I too came here to get married. I hope my future husband is honest!"

21 |

The three weeks at the boarding house passed quickly. Dikran told Lydia that he had given up his goal of becoming a missionary. Lydia was disappointed to hear that. Mrs. Sarkissian had emphasized that goal as reflecting what a good man he was. Lydia wondered about his honesty. She felt better after he explained that he had decided to give priority to a stable family life; to supporting his wife, to being a good husband and father. He had given up his job at the bakery to become a tram driver in central London. That, he told Lydia, allowed him stable employment and a good income. He would look after her well.

After giving Lydia two days to catch up on sleep, he visited her each morning. He had arranged for the wedding to take place on October eighteenth, and he was determined that they would get to know each other well beforehand. The first few days they went for walks in the immediate neighbourhood. He showed her where he lived from the outside of the building. Knowing that she too would live there soon, Lydia was pleased to see that his flat was in a nice-looking house on a street that was cleaner than many they had passed. She noted also that there were some shops and a small park close by. But nothing was familiar. She was overwhelmed with the noise, the busyness, and the greyness. It was difficult adjusting. The large urban environment, the different languages she heard spoken, the different climate and being surrounded by strangers all made her nervous. She still did not know if her family was dead or alive. She continued to miss them all intensely.

Dikran was aware of how unsettled Lydia was feeling. He recalled how alienated he had felt when he first came to London.

"Lydia," he said, hoping to help her feel less anxious, "on Sunday we will go to the Armenian church. The building is only two years old, but it's traditional and modelled after the bell tower of the Haghpat Monastery in Armenia. I think you will like it."

She did. Entering the church, Lydia felt her whole body relax and felt like she could breathe for the first time since arriving in London. The last time Lydia had been in an Armenian church had been over ten years previously in Zeitun, but she recalled everything about the service. She crossed herself upon entering, kissed the hand of the priest, took holy communion, and shared in the holy bread.

What she found most evocative was the censing—the practice of swinging a censor suspended from chains among the participants in the service. The sweet smell of the incense brought tears to her eyes as it took her back to her childhood. She hoped that the rising smoke would carry her prayers for the safety of her family to heaven.

"We'll be back for our wedding," Dikran told her, as they left. Her smile at him was broad and genuine. "And my dear Lydia, you see there are many Armenians in London. In fact, the church was built by Mr. Gulbenkian as a gathering place for the deported Armenians, like us, who are now living in London. We'll make friends here, yes?"

"Thank you, Dikran." She touched his arm lightly. "Thank you." For the first time since the last day she had spent with her parents, Lydia felt understood. She started to relax in Dikran's presence.

The next morning, Dikran asked Lydia what she would most like to see.

"Grass, trees, flowers, and animals", was her immediate reply.

"Okay," he said, "I know just the place." He grinned at her in a way that made her nervous. Was he hiding something? She soon discovered what.

To get to Regent's Park—their destination—they would have to travel the underground railway. Dikran was not sure how Lydia would react to such an experience. As it turned out, not well. She was fine walking to the station but then horrified having to travel deep below the ground level into a dark, smelly tunnel. Before she could turn and leave, a train came roaring to a halt in front of her. Dikran took her hand and ensured she step into the carriage with its wooden slatted floor and wooden seating. Lydia shook with fear and held Dikran's hand. After what seemed an interminable time but was no more than fifteen minutes, they shuddered to the third stop of their journey where Dikran said they should get off. A sign said Baker Street Station. They stepped out quickly and watched the train roar off down the tunnel. Lydia was still shaking and still clutching Dikran's hand.

"It's fine—we'll be somewhere wonderful very soon," he told her. "We just have to go up the escalators here."

"Up the what?" she asked, trying to avoid hyperventilating.

"Come, I'll show you."

They walked along the track until they came to the base of a steep wooden escalator which was grinding its way noisily upward. Lydia could not see the top of it. She stared at it, bewildered. Before moving on to a step, she watched others.

"Don't let go of me," she pleaded with Dikran, as they got on. Up it went, jerking and making kerthunk kerthunk kerthunk sounds all the way. Would they never reach the top, Lydia wondered?

"You just rode on the oldest underground railway in the whole world. It's been going since 1863," Dikran told her, as they finally exited onto the street. Lydia let go of his hand, took a deep breath, and looked around. They were very close to what looked like an enormous park. She now understood their journey.

Putting his hand on Lydia's elbow, Dikran said he would now be her tour guide.

"Tell me about the park, then," she replied.

Dikran explained that Regent's Park was even older than the underground railway. It had been constructed for royalty but was opened to the public way back in 1835. Lydia was intrigued by the different types of trees that lined the walkways. They were a different shape, size, and shade of green from those she had been familiar with as a child. She was delighted by the beauty of the water-lily house and fascinated with the boating lake.

"Can we go on the lake?" she asked.

"Not today. There is something else here I want to show you."

"Is it safe to go on this lake?"

"Yes." As they continued walking, Dikran elaborated. "Well, most of the time. Back in the winter of 1867, this lake had iced over—it must have been a worse than usual winter. Anyway, a lot of people were on the ice when it collapsed. I think it was about forty who died, but hundreds fell in and were okay. After that they drained it and when they refilled it, they just went to four feet—so now if you did fall in you could easily stand up."

While he was telling her this, they arrived at where he was taking her —the zoo. Lydia was thrilled. She felt sad for a moment as she thought about how much Luke would have enjoyed the zoo. But she found the animals too enchanting to stay sad—the oryx, the kudus, and especially the orangutan. She stopped in awe at the enclosure of a large American black bear called Winnipeg.

"That's an odd name, isn't it? Dikran?"

"I s'pose, but she was a gift from Canada and that's the name of the place there that she came from. She's incredibly tame—she even lets kids ride on her."

"You seem to know everything." Lydia said teasingly.

"Well, I read up so I could impress you." Dikran replied, smiling at her, "and I have one more fact to tell you about Winnie as she's called. I found out that a children's author, a Mr. Milne, used to take his son Christopher to see Winnie, and last year he published a poem about her. The poem is called "Teddy Bear." I can remember only the beginning— do you want to hear it?"

"Please."

Dikran recited.

A bear, however hard he tries,

Grows tubby without exercise.
Our Teddy Bear is short and fat,
Which is not to be wondered at;
He gets what exercise he can
By falling off the ottoman,
But generally seems to lack
The energy to clamber back.

"Now I have to take you home and get to work. We'll use the new bus this time. You'll see it in a minute. These buses have just started running here."

Lydia was intrigued by the bright red double-decker bus that pulled up soon after they arrived at the stop. She had seen a few around since arriving in the city, but had not thought about riding in one.

They climbed the narrow winding stairs to the upper deck and Lydia was too absorbed by the view it afforded to feel nervous. It had been a good morning.

22

The outings with Dikran were enjoyable. They helped Lydia get to know the city, and to begin to trust Dikran. But they did little to ease the difficulties of adjustment or the loss of her family. And they did nothing to ease her fears of the sexual intimacy that would be required of her after the wedding. Long talks with Eva in the evenings were of somewhat more help. Lydia expressed her fears of what Dikran would want from her physically. Eva told Lydia that she had experienced sexual intimacy and that in the context of a loving relationship and marriage, it should be enjoyable. It was not something to be afraid of. Lydia was shocked and puzzled by the revelation that her friend had engaged in sexual behaviour outside of marriage.

Whenever possible, they would sit together in the communal living room by the fireplace and reminisce about their childhoods. They shared their heartache at the loss of family, their sense that they did not belong anywhere, and their anxieties about their futures. Lydia soon felt comfortable enough to discuss some of her experiences with the Aydin and Yuvuz families. She did not talk about the rapes. Over time, they moved from discussing their pasts to talking about their futures. Eva wanted to move beyond being a victim of circumstances. She wanted a job that was interesting and paid enough for her to live a decent life, or to meet a nice man, marry and have a family.

"But it'll be a while 'til I trust anyone after what happened," she concluded. "What about you, Lydia? What are you hoping for?"

"It is in God's hands, I believe. He has sent me here to marry Dikran Vartounian, so that is what I must do. So far, her seems like a kind man, but… anyway, I am hoping that he will be a good Christian, that he won't drink or gamble, that he'll be faithful to me, and that he'll be a good provider."

"But what about you?" Eva asked.

"I'll do my best to be a good wife and mother. I'll try to make our home comfortable. I already know how to sew and clean, and I'll learn how to cook properly. I remember how my mother used to make the cabbage dolmas. I used to help her. I wonder if I can remember how to make them?" She paused, sighing. "But Eva," she continued, "it's hard, everything is so different, everything. I'm so glad I knew the language before I came, otherwise it would be impossible."

Lydia was content enough to stay at the boarding house with Eva. However, more quickly than she could have expected, it was October eighteenth—the day of her wedding. Dikran had obtained the marriage licence, booked the church, and purchased rings for himself and for Lydia. All was well organized.

Trembling with fear and praying for strength, Lydia put on the white wedding gown that Eva had helped her find in a used clothing store. She had been hesitant to wear white given that it was the colour of purity and her tattoos made it plain that she was not pure. But Eva, who had assumed from Lydia's history that she probably had been raped, had explained that wearing white for her wedding at St. Sarkis was a way of moving beyond her past abuse. It was not sinful.

"It'll symbolize a new pure start," she insisted, "like the past never happened. You look beautiful Lydia. Do you have Dikran's ring? Come, it's time for us to go."

Dikran's best man, his close friend, Raffi Kevorkian, was also a member of the same Armenian church. Raffi worked in construction but was hoping to become a tram driver like Dikran. The two men were at the altar when Lydia and Eva arrived. Lydia found the music and the smell of the incense calming. She thanked God for keeping her safe, for allowing this wedding of two Armenians who could so easily have been killed along with their families and friends, and for giving her a fresh start with Dikran.

Lydia had never attended a wedding, other than the simple service of Paul and Sarah, so did not know what to expect other than what Eva had talked to her about. She found the ceremony serious and impressive. As Eva had described, there were the traditional Bible readings and hymns, and the reciting of the Lord's Prayer—all in Armenian. These she was familiar with, but there was so much more. Knowing how unfamiliar the rituals were to Lydia, the priest explained the meaning of each step. They were asked to join hands for the exchange of vows as a symbol of their oneness. The exchange of rings, after each was blessed by the priest, signified that each of them would be enriched by their union.

The climax of the service, and a ritual Lydia found particularly fascinating, was the rite of crowning. Lydia and Dikran were crowned as a sign of the glory and honour God was bestowing on them as just and wise rulers of their own home. The blessing and drinking of wine from the common cup was to emphasize that from the moment of marriage on, the couple would share all the joys and sorrows of their lives. Finally, they reached the benediction. The priest blessed them once again and asked God to protect them. It was over. Lydia was now Mrs. Dikran Vartounian.

There would be no honeymoon trip, but Dikran had taken a week off work. He hoped this would be enough to help Lydia adjust to her new life with him. He quickly realized that it would not. She was all right when they first were at Dikran's home, because Raffi and Eva had come with them to share a celebratory meal. But after their friends left and as bedtime approached, Lydia became increasingly agitated and tearful.

She went into the small bathroom to change into the nightgown Eva had given her as a wedding present. She was feeling alone and lost. Her homesickness was more intense than it had ever been, her loss of family more painful, and her fear of what was to come great. She asked God's forgiveness for her doubts and fears and prayed for the strength to be a good wife. She hoped Eva was right and that she could be intimate with Dikran.

When she climbed into the double bed and lay beside Dikran, she was shaking uncontrollably. Using every ounce of patience he could muster, Dikran talked to her quietly and stroked her hair. He asked if he could hold her, and she reluctantly agreed. He did not make any effort to touch her intimately, but simply held her until she fell asleep. Two hours later, she woke up screaming. She was experiencing a flashback with vivid, distressing images of her last few nights as Hayriye.

23

Dikran did not know the details of what had happened to Lydia, but he knew that most of those in her situation had been raped. Her tattoos and her behaviour strongly indicated that Lydia was indeed a victim of rape, likely frequently and by more than one man. He sensed her reluctance to be touched soon after he picked her up from the ship. He understood and respected it, but more than ever now that they were married, he wanted to help her move beyond it.

Dikran recalled the horrors he and his mother had witnessed during their journey to Yerevan. He recalled his mother's wailing when his brother died. He had promised God at that point that if he and his mother were safe, he would do whatever he could to help other Armenian women, especially those who had been abused. He believed it was God's will that he help Lydia heal and he felt blessed to have that opportunity. When Lydia woke up screaming, he calmed her by talking softly and holding her. He stressed his respect for her feelings.

"Lydia," he said. "I understand why you don't want to be touched and I will never force you. I will wait until you are ready, whether that takes a day, a week, or a few months."

"I feel so ashamed, so full of sin." Lydia replied sobbing. "But I want to be a good wife to you."

"None of what happened to you was your fault, Lydia, and there is nothing sinful about married couples loving each other."

When she awoke the next morning, Lydia felt guilty not only about her past but also about refusing Dikran. She didn't really want to talk about it, but after a week of nightly nightmares, she decided to talk again to Eva. She divulged more than she had during their previous chats, but it remained difficult for her to talk more fully about what had happened to her. She described how she was afraid she would again lose control over her body, and how vulnerable she felt. It was cathartic to reveal her fears, if not the details of her experiences.

"I totally understand." Eva was sympathetic. "But you can't avoid sexual intercourse forever, Lydia. You both want children, don't you? More than that, though, sex shouldn't just be a means to an end or an obligation of marriage, Lydia. It should be pleasurable. There is such a vast difference between sexual assault—what happened to you—and making love."

They talked several times over the next few weeks, and Lydia prayed for guidance and for strength. Dikran continued to reassure her that he was willing to wait until she was ready. Six weeks went by before she felt able to initiate any physical contact with him. As soon as he responded, she found herself dissociating, as she had with Okan Yavuz and his sons. She felt disconnected not only from her own body, but also from Dikran. She forced herself to remain connected and fought the immediate sense of panic. It was difficult. She would often ask Dikran to stop touching her and would then feel guilty about rejecting him. He remained patient.

It took time and effort, but as she developed increasing trust in Dikran, and their mutual respect and emotional intimacy built, she became able to have intercourse without dread. It took many more months during which she became confident that Dikran would never do anything she didn't want and would stop any time she asked him to before she finally could experience pleasure. She realized, to her delight and satisfaction, that Eva was right. Making love felt good, physically and emotionally. It helped her feel closer to Dikran. She felt more confident in herself and her relationship. It was a wonderful realization that she was able to drop the mantle of victimhood, to put behind her the abuse and the rapes.

Feeling at peace and settled, Lydia wrote long detailed letters to Sarah and to Mrs. Sarkissian telling them about Dikran, Eva, and London. She asked each if they had any news from Armenia and asked Mrs. Sarkissian if she had located Luke. The replies were friendly, but there was no news of Luke and sad news from Sarah. Sarah informed Lydia that her husband, Paul, had died after being hit by a car less than three months after they had moved to Constantinople. Her life had changed markedly, she wrote to Lydia, but she was doing well given the circumstances and was considering a new beginning—perhaps moving somewhere else and getting employment.

Lydia continued her weekly lunches with Eva that had started soon after her arrival in London. She was delighted when Eva told her that she was dating Raffi and that they were getting along very well. After her previous experience, Eva was impressed with Raffi's sincerity. She trusted him.

The four began to meet every Sunday at St. Sarkis. After the service, they would go for lunch to a small nearby café and, as often as they could, they would then go for walks in one of London's parks. Lydia and Eva particularly enjoyed going to Hyde Park.

They would usually stop to see who was orating, or pontificating, as Raffi would say, at Speaker's Corner. It was busiest and most interesting on Sundays. Dikran told Lydia that it was a designated place that anyone could use to talk about almost anything. Even famous people like Karl Marx and Lenin had spoken there often, he said.

"There are two basic rules, though," he explained. "You aren't allowed to use obscene language and you have to be prepared for hecklers."

"What's hecklers?" Lydia asked.

Raffi explained to Lydia that the role of the listening members of the public had become one of shouting disagreements and interrupting the speaker with derisive comments. "All in fun, well, mostly," he added.

After the marriage, at Lydia's request, Dikran worked mostly day shifts. He picked up a late shift when he could, since he was trying to save enough to buy them a house. But he always came home for dinner.

Lydia started each day by going to the shops to buy food for their meals. The availability of a wide variety of foods impressed her, but she thought longingly of the fresh olives and figs that she had enjoyed as a child. There were none in London. She would then spend the rest of the day on household chores and cooking their dinner. She never resented the domestic chores. Cleaning and cooking for herself and Dikran was meaningful and pleasurable. It was not at all like her earlier servitude.

As she became more used to London, and when Dikran was at work, Lydia went for long walks in the neighbourhood. She tried to be friendly with the neighbours, but aside from a curt response to her greetings, they looked at her askance and acted as though she were some sort of monster. She had experienced little disdain or discrimination from the shopkeepers, so this surprised her. It intensified her homesickness.

She missed Zeitun and, above all, she missed her family. She also missed Sarah, Mrs. Sarkissian, and all the children she had been working with at the camp. Playing the piano to accompany the children as they sang hymns had been enjoyable. She would sit sometimes in her living room, or the park on rare sunny days, recalling all the good parts of living in the orphanage and in the camps. She was the most homesick and lonely on the many winter days when London was obliterated by pea-soup fog. Lydia would close her eyes and recall as best she could the clear mountains and the rushing river of Zeitun.

* * *

The fog, like the pea soup after which it was called, was thick and yellowish, although some days it was more green than yellow and sometimes it was even black. There were days when the fog was so thick that she could barely see her feet when she stepped outside. Her eyes itched and she coughed uncontrollably. The first time she asked Dikran about the fog, he explained that the main cause of it was the use of coal for heating.

"The fog hurts because it's full of coal dust," he said.

"It's so hard to breathe when it's like that," she commented.

"You're right," Dikran replied, "I read that they got some new instruments—don't know what they are—but apparently, they showed that there is three hundred and forty thousand pieces of soot in every cubic inch of air you breathe on these foggy days. Hard to fathom that. Best to stay in."

"Can't they do anything about it?" Lydia asked.

"Only if people stop using coal. There are a lot of people arguing for a switch to gas instead of coal, but so far..." He shrugged.

* * *

In the summer of 1927, Raffi and Eva got married, and moved to a house even closer to Dikran and Lydia than the boarding house where Eva had lived. Lydia was thrilled to have her friend close enough to visit every day if she wanted. Dikran was pleased to see his friend so happy and settled down with a good Christian Armenian woman—almost as good as Lydia, he thought to himself.

December came with even better news for the Vartounians. Many mornings in November, Lydia had awoken feeling sick. She recalled her mother talking about her Aunt Ruth's morning sickness early in the pregnancy and wondered if it was possible that she was pregnant. In early December, she noticed that her breasts were sore, and her abdominal area was getting bigger despite the daily walks. A doctor's visit confirmed her pregnancy.

Dikran could not have been more pleased or more excited. Lydia was both thrilled and nervous. The baby was due to be born in early June of 1928. Dikran vowed he would find them a house with a garden before then. He asked Lydia what she would most like to have in her new house.

Without hesitating, she answered, "A piano."

24

As she prepared her children—five-year-old Leon and two-year-old Miriam—for a visit to the London Zoo at Regent's Park, Lydia thought about how the past five years with her family had been her happiest since her childhood in 'the before', as she thought of it. Moving into a new neighbourhood on the edge of the city and setting up a house and looking after babies had been challenging. She missed living close to Eva. But the difficulties were more than offset by the joy of having her own home and family, a piano, and a garden large enough to have a play space for the children and for Lydia to grow vegetables. There was so much to thank God for, Lydia thought each day. But despite her overall contentment, there remained several nights a month when traumatic memories disturbed her.

On those nights, Lydia would wake in the early hours of the morning covered in sweat from dreams in which she could clearly see and hear the horrors of a baby being beaten to death, or thrown in a river, or hear the screams of an Armenian orphan girl killed because she had dysentery and was slowing the march or hear the endless sobbing of the girls who were raped. She relived her time with the Yavuz family. It was all so real. It was hard for her to believe that fifteen years had passed since she escaped and ended up at the orphanage in Aleppo. Lydia's screams often woke Dikran. He would hold her until she calmed. He encouraged her to talk about the past atrocities, hoping it would help.

Lydia remained too uncomfortable with her body and her sexuality to talk about her experiences with Dikran. Several times she had tried to talk more with Eva, but either her or Eva's children would always be present. Although they all played well together, they were too young to be unattended.

A month ago, she had written to Sarah, describing her experiences with flashbacks and nightmares, and asking Sarah if she also had any similar experiences. Lydia checked the post daily for a response.

In her reply, which came almost two months later, Sarah wrote mostly about her new life. She described how moving to Marseille, where there was a large Armenian community, had helped her recover from the loss of Paul. She wrote at length about how much she enjoyed her experiences as a teacher of seven-year-olds. Toward the end of the letter, she expressed her dismay at hearing of Lydia's continuing nightmares. Reading of them, she noted, revived her own. They must, she emphasized to Lydia, put the past behind them.

* * *

"Aren't we going?" asked Leon, impatiently tugging on Lydia's dress and interrupting her reverie. "I wanna see Winnie."

"Yes, I just have to put Miri's boots on her, and get my hat."

Before putting her hat on, Lydia checked out her new hairstyle. Recently, she had her hair cut and styled for the first time since she was a child. Her long braids had become dated and were unattractive at her age. She looked approvingly at her new chin length hair with its side part and soft waves. She felt a moment of guilt for admiring herself in a mirror. That was sinful. "Forgive my vanity, Lord." she said.

As they walked to the bus stop, Lydia was, as usual, confronted with hostile stares from some of her neighbours. She was never sure whether their suspicion of, or animosity to, her was personal or resulted from a general antipathy to refugees and immigrants. Doing her best to turn the other cheek and be a good Christian, she always said "Good morning" to each as they passed. Few responded.

Arriving at the zoo, Leon ran ahead to the bear pit. Miriam, seeing where they were, said, "Bear mummy, bear." Winnie had just had her nineteenth birthday. The remnants of her party were still visible.

The children had brought her a treat—some condensed milk. Because Winnie was such a tame bear, the children were allowed to go into the pit and hand-feed her. Before they left, they each hugged the bear.

Dikran had purchased the 1926 book *Winnie the Pooh* and the 1928 *The House at Pooh Corner* for the children. He read from one or the other book each night. Lydia thought it would be more appropriate for the children to hear Bible stories, but seeing them cuddled with their father, who despite being tired in the evenings always enjoyed reading to them, brought her great pleasure. She would reflect on how sacrosanct family was, how precious for children to live with their parents. She could and did tell them Bible stories in the daytime when their father was at work.

Lydia was surprised to see another letter from Sarah when they got home. Both children were tired from the outing, so she settled them for a nap and opened the letter.

Marseille, August 05,1933.

My dear Lydia:

As I mentioned before, I am so sorry to hear you are still plagued with nightmares, tho it's good to hear you are having them less often. I find being in Marseille and being part of the Armenian community here has helped me in so many ways. I am so pleased that I moved here. It's great to be in a place with so many of our countrymen. I didn't know before that there've been Armenians here since the fifteenth century. But there've been boatloads arriving over the past few years. I pretty much feel at home!

The real reason I am writing this letter—so soon after the last one—is that I wanted to ask what you have heard about Mr. Hitler in Germany. I wonder if you have heard how much unrest there is in Germany and how difficult it is for the Jewish peoples. I am worried about it spilling over into France. But what has really scared me is that one of our church members brought a copy of Mein Kampf—the book that Hitler wrote when he was in jail. I read the book and I think he is an evil man, Lydia, like Talat Pasha. He has a strong belief that his race is superior and that the Jews should be got rid of. Sound familiar? He describes races other than his own—the Aryan (not people like you and me, of course, my dear friend)—as "a parasite within the nation" and "the destroyer of culture." And can you believe it, now he is chancellor of Germany!! I am wondering if the Jews will have to leave Germany like we had to leave Armenia—do you think they will come here to Marseille, or maybe they will go to London? All this turmoil at the same time as there are problems with the economy and lots of people losing their jobs. I just don't know if I can face anymore problems. As you know, it has been only recently that I have been able to really relax and enjoy my life. Do tell me what you have heard, Lydia—perhaps your Mr. MacDonald has explained things on the BBC radio?

On a happier note, I was glad to read that your dear children are doing well, and that dear Dikran still has his job. I expect you are keeping busy with your family and the church. Please write again soon. And I do hope your nightmares are gone.

25

By 1938, Lydia's nightmares worried her less than other concerns. "You know, Dikran," she said, at the end of a particularly challenging day, "Sarah predicted this horror we are seeing now five years ago. It seemed so far away and impossible then."

"I think it stems from the job and financial difficulties you and I have been blessed to escape. People have been so scared and uncertain about how they're to live, and so many lost their jobs." Dikran paused for a moment. Sighing, he continued. "You know they've turned to the worst possible leaders just because they've promised prosperity. People like Hitler."

"I'm worried. Leon's been having problems at school with other children calling him a 'dirty Jew' if you can believe that. They told him to go back to where he came from. Can you believe that little ten-year-old boys can be so cruel! God help us."

"Has Miriam been bothered also?" Dikran sounded upset.

"Miriam hasn't said anything," Lydia said, "but she's got the same Armenian nose and dark features as Leon. I wouldn't be surprised if the other children call her names too. She hasn't been as keen to go to school recently. And what's maybe even worse is that both children have told me recently that the others tease them about their mum having a blue face."

Dikran noticed that Lydia was increasingly distraught. He took her hand. She gripped it. After taking a deep breath, she continued.

"They asked if I was a monster. Leon asked me again about my face, but I just don't want to talk about it. I can't talk about it. I just told him I had a little accident when I was a child. I trust God will forgive me for telling a lie. How horrible children can be, Dikran. I just don't know how to protect Miri and Leon. I keep praying for guidance."

Dikran put his arm around Lydia. "They'll be okay. Never forget," he said "our children have us. They have a mother and a father who love them and care for them, they have a proper home and family. We didn't have that, Lydia. Nothing's more precious than family. And let's be thankful that they're not Jewish children—things would be much worse."

Dikran turned and picked up the newspaper. Lydia knew from experience that this meant he did not wish to talk anymore. She thought of it as his "leave me in peace" signal. But she continued.

"How? And why are they calling our son, or anyone, a dirty Jew?"

"There's no way to justify it of course, but you know it's been an awful winter for cold and snow, and as I mentioned before, so many people are losing money or losing jobs. People are feeling unhappy and angry at others. I think many people are looking for someone to blame for their problems. Seems they've targeted the Jews. The children pick up on it. It's complicated and I'm tired Lydia, let's leave it for now." He picked up the paper again.

Lydia learned more the following Sunday. The newspaper had forecast an ideal August day with warm temperatures and clear skies. It turned out to be even nicer. Lydia and Eva had planned a picnic lunch for after the church service. Lydia had made some derev dolma—stuffed grape leaves from the vines growing in her garden, and some tourshi —mixed pickles. Eva brought some boerags—phyllo pastry triangles stuffed with feta cheese and spinach, some khourabia—shortbread cookies, and some fresh oranges.

They went from St. Sarkis church to Regent's Park. After they finished eating, Miriam asked if they could go to see Winnie. Lydia gently reminded her that Winnie had gone to heaven. She suggested they play on the swings that were beside the picnic area while the grown-ups had a chat, and then they could all go to the zoo.

Eva and Raffi were anxious to tell Lydia and Dikran about their new neighbours who were refugees from Germany. The Krasnors, Klaus and Gretel, were a well-educated young couple who said they were thrilled to have been able to settle in London. In getting to know them, Raffi said, they had learned a lot.

"It's like this," said Raffi. "Jews aren't wanted in Germany and haven't been for some time." Many Jews, the Krasnors had explained, left Germany when Hitler came into power some five years ago. Since then, things had only got worse for Jews as well as other minorities. The Nazi government had been passing anti-Jewish legislation, and there was increasing violence against Jews.

"What sort of legislation?" asked Dikran.

"What the Krasnors explained," Raffi responded, "was that led by Hitler, the Nazis did whatever they could to eliminate Jews from the professional and cultural life of Germany."

"And," added Eva, "from economics—apparently thousands of them lost their jobs or their businesses."

"Why?" asked Lydia. "Just a minute. I need to check on the children." They had been playing hide and go seek, and she had been unable to see Miriam for a few moments. She returned, and Raffi explained.

The Krasnors had told them that in 1933, at a Nazi rally in Nuremberg, new laws had been passed: the Reich Citizenship Law, and the Law for the Protection of German Blood and German Honour.

"The name says enough." Dikran commented. "Goodness!"

The laws, Raffi said, were based on the belief Hitler had imbued in the party that Jews were an inferior race who must be kept apart from Aryans to avoid contaminating the gene pool. With these Nuremberg Laws, the Jews essentially lost their status as citizens of Germany and all the accompanying rights of German citizenship.

"So, they had to leave? We know too well how painful it is to have to leave your homeland." Lydia commented. "Where did they all go? Did many of them come here to the UK?"

The answer was interrupted by a child's scream. They looked toward the play area and saw that a little girl had fallen off a swing. Miriam ran to comfort her. Lydia went to check on the child and praise Miriam for being helpful. The girl's mother arrived and comforted the frightened but unhurt child. Lydia returned to the group, and the conversation continued.

Eva explained that restrictions under the Aliens Act meant that few had been allowed in. Although, she had heard that the crazy Doctor Freud had been allowed to emigrate to London with his family. Apparently, his daughter had been arrested and interrogated by the Nazis, and the Nazis had burned all Freud's books. He had left Vienna and brought his family to London.

"Probably a good idea to burn his books," Lydia interrupted Eva. "Isn't he the one that wrote all that sinful stuff about, you know, dirty things?" She still could not bring herself to say sex.

Eva, ignoring Lydia's comment, continued to explain that to get into England, you had to have a job or a guarantor, otherwise you would only be granted a transit visa which meant you could only stay for a month on the way to somewhere else.

"Where else?" asked Dikran.

"That was and I guess still is among the worst parts of the whole thing, the Krasnors told us." Eva said. "You explain Raffi."

"Okay. Well, apparently the Jews were in an awful bind because they were supposed to leave Germany, but no one wanted them. I read up on it a bit at the library after we chatted with the Krasnors, and it's really sad. The UK didn't really want them to come here, but nowhere else wanted them either. Nowhere in Europe, or the United States, or Canada, or it seems anywhere. There was a conference just last month in Evian in France where I think it was thirty or thirty-two countries met to decide what to do about all the folks having to leave Nazi Germany. They agreed they needed to be accepted somewhere, but none wanted them. No one was willing to loosen their immigration restrictions. In fact, I remember a quote from the article I was reading. It was from someone, I forget his name, Weimer or maybe Weizman. I do recall he was a Russian biochemist. Anyway, what he said about the conference stuck with me. He said, 'the world seemed to be divided into two parts—those places where Jews could not live and those that they could not enter.'"

"What were they supposed to do?" asked Dikran. "just travel around for the rest of their lives. It's ridiculous; it's unholy!"

"What can we do to help?" Lydia asked immediately. "We all know what it's like to be persecuted. We were lucky to be able to come to the UK, just think if no one had wanted us anywhere. It's too awful."

An answer came later that year.

Lydia was exhausted. The ongoing radio and newspaper reports about what was happening to the Jews in German were painful. Once again, flashbacks tormented her several nights a week. The flashbacks remained vivid. She could see, hear, feel, and even smell everything that had happened that last night before she escaped the Yavuz family.

One night, the nightmare was so real she found herself checking her genitals when she awoke, to see if there was evidence of damage. She wondered if she was going crazy. She stayed awake the rest of the night, terrified of what she might experience if she went back to sleep. Her mood did not improve when Miriam spilled her glass of milk on the kitchen floor at breakfast. The mess and the waste of nutrition were equally upsetting. She bit her lip to prevent her from screaming at Miriam. She was glad when the children had left for school and Dikran left for work.

Going to the shops to buy meat for the evening meal was a challenge. As well as her exhaustion, she had to contend with a very heavy fog and air so thick she found breathing difficult. She was struggling to get home with her bag of meat and vegetables, hardly able to see a few inches in front of her, when a man bumped into her. In her heightened state of exhaustion and anxiety, she panicked. She dropped her bag and ran, but with the lack of visibility and in her panic, she ran right into a phone booth and fell over. She lay on the ground sobbing.

"It's okay Mrs. Vartounian. It's just me, your neighbour Nigel Taylor. You must've met my wife, Janet. We live across the street from you. I'm so sorry I bumped into you. This darn fog. Can't see a thing.

Are you hurt? Let me help you up. I think I can see where you are. Come on, love, you know I won't hurt you."

Reluctantly, Lydia allowed him to hold her arm and help her get up. He suggested she wait where she was while he found her shopping and then guide her home.

"Lived here all my life," he said. "Kinda used to this bloody pea soup, especially in November."

* * *

Dikran was also having a rough day. He was on an earlier than usual shift. The morning was cold, damp, and foggy. Driving the tram in the fog was an extraordinary challenge, but one he could handle. It helped that the fog was not quite as dense on the route he was driving as it had been when he left home. What he had more difficulty with was the conversation between two passengers who were sitting directly behind him. They had started out complaining about the Prime Minister, Mr. Chamberlain. They thought he was weak and not doing enough to keep England for the British.

"All these good English people without jobs," one passenger said, "and that arsehole lets aliens come in and take them."

"You got it, mate," said his friend. "All these so-called refugees—who's paying for 'em, that's what I wanna know. Their housing, health care, teaching 'em to speak proper English."

The conversation continued to denigrate refugees and non-whites until the passengers got off the tram, which was about twenty minutes later. The only thing that kept Dikran from confronting them and telling them to get off his tram was the certain knowledge that he would lose his job if he did. That, he could not afford. But he was sorely tempted to do so, and by the time they dismounted the tram, he was shaking with anger. His anger dissipated during his walk home at the end of his shift. It was revived when the children came home from school at four thirty.

Leon had a torn shirt and a black eye. Dikran and Lydia were shocked. Leon had always been a quiet and obedient child. He got along well with others, children, and adults, but was equally content by himself. More than once, his schoolteachers had commented that he was the ideal child: a hard worker, an achiever, a kind and friendly child. Dikran immediately pressed him to tell what happened.

Leon did not want to explain but eventually caved to pressure from his parents, who assured him they would not be angry. He described a pattern of bullying that had escalated over the past two weeks. There were two boys in his class who taunted him endlessly about his mother's blue face. Over the past week, they had followed him around chanting 'your mum's an alien, and you're a feckin Jew, you look like a scallion, and you stink of pooh.'

"I didn't mean to hit him," Leon sobbed. "I'm sorry."

"You boys are only ten years old, and they speak like that?" Dikran was appalled.

Lydia sat beside Leon, hugging him and stroking his hair. "It's okay, Leon" she said. "Those boys must be very unhappy to be so mean. And you," she said, turning to Miriam, "what's got you looking so upset?"

"It's not fair," Miriam said. "The other kids made me giggle while teacher was talking, and I got yelled at. I was the only one even though it wasn't my fault. And now teacher says that I must write lines. She wants me to write 'I will not giggle in class' fifty times. That's going to take ages. I hate her." Lydia sighed. Do all parents have one child who is easy and one who is always in trouble, she wondered. She could not recall such problems when she and Luke were young.

Lydia called the family for dinner, and after Leon said grace, she served each a steaming hot bowl of lamb stew. Despite their moods, they all ate heartily. Lydia was pleased there was no waste. She did not mind spending hours shopping and cooking if her family enjoyed their meals as they had tonight. Looking at the empty bowls, she felt better than she had all day.

"I have an idea," Lydia said. "Now that we have finished eating, let's each talk about something we are thankful for. I'll start. I thank God for each of you—my wonderful family. I love each of you very, very much."

"And I also thank God for my lovely wife and wonderful children," said Dikran. "Your turn, Leon, what do you thank God for?"

Leon looked uncomfortable and then blurted out, "I'm glad I hit George today, even though I know I'm not supposed to. But it felt good to see him cry."

"Well," Dikran said with a smile, "at least you're honest. I think God probably understands, don't you Lydia?" She did not answer, but she could not resist a smile.

"My turn. I'm glad I only have to write fifty lines. Yesterday, Lisa had to write a hundred. But I am not thankful for my teacher. Can I be excused now?"

Once the children settled for the night, and the dishes were done, Dikran suggested that they relax together by listening to the BBC on their radio. Lydia hoped there would be a music broadcast. She especially enjoyed the organ concerts from St. Georges Hall in the city. Although the organ was in a theatre, she always imagined that the organ was in a church and the organist was playing to glorify God. There was no music that night. Instead, the announcer informed listeners that there was to be a play: *Murder in the Cathedral*, a verse drama by T.S. Eliot.

"What's it about, Dikran, do you know?"

"It's about the assassination of Thomas Becket in Canterbury Cathedral. Something that happened back in 1170, so you don't need to get upset about it, Lydia."

Although not keen to listen to anything to do with murder, Lydia agreed to listen for a few minutes and see how she felt. She need not have worried. The play had hardly started when there was an announcement that ended the presentation of the play.

There were reports, perhaps leaked by someone in government, that there had been a spate of antisemitic violence in Europe, resulting in widespread violence. Dikran turned the volume up and they listened to the sketchy details that were provided. "It seems," the BBC announcer said, "like it was a night of broken glass. Our information is that the German propaganda minister, Goebbels, declared that the Jews had conspired to assassinate the German ambassador Herr Ernst Von Roth. This accusation," he continued, "appears to have led to the destruction of hundreds of synagogues, community centres, homes, and businesses, by members of the Nazi Party, Storm Troopers, and the Hitler Youth. At this time, we do not have information on when this destruction happened, but it is likely that it was within the past month. We are told that shattered glass from broken windows lined the streets. There was extensive looting, and many citizens were injured. We have no information on possible deaths. Reports are that the worst hit areas were the cities of Berlin and Vienna. We emphasize that this report is not yet confirmed," the announcer concluded, "but it is from a generally reliable source. We shall update you as we obtain more information. We do not believe there is any reason for British Jews to be concerned at this time. And now back to our regular programming."

27

Lydia had a harder time than usual sleeping that night. The nightmares were even more vivid. Not again, she thought upon waking. It can't be. She hoped she had dreamt about the broken glass, the looting, the violence. But it was real. In reading the newspapers over the next few days, she discovered that the antisemitic violence in Germany and Austria was worse than the BBC announcer had initially described.

The newspapers reported that more than a thousand synagogues had been burned while firefighters made no effort to save them, although they worked hard to save adjacent buildings if they were not owned by Jews. It was also reported that thousands of Jewish businesses had been vandalized or destroyed. So had many schools, homes, hospitals, and even cemeteries. The death toll from the riots was already up to ninety-one, and it was reported that thousands of Jewish men had been sent to concentration camps. Lydia felt a growing sense of despair and helplessness as she learned more about what the papers were now calling the night of broken glass—Kristallnacht. She prayed for guidance and that God would not let others have to suffer as the Armenians did. She prayed that her father and Luke had somehow stayed safe.

Talking with Dikran after the children had gone to bed the next night, Lydia had a fuller understanding of what had happened but was no less disturbed by it. She was pleased that they had planned to meet with the Kevorkians the next day. Lydia looked forward to being able to discuss the situation with Eva and hoped that Eva would have some comforting information.

"Do you think Raffi may know more from the Krasnors?" Lydia asked Dikran. "There must be something we can do. I can't bear it, Dikran. After what we went through...."

Dikran put the radio on to see if there was any further news. They were just in time to hear the former Prime Minister, Stanley Baldwin, issue a plea for donations in support of the Lord Baldwin Fund for Refugees. He also proposed a ten percent tax on the sale of movie and theatre tickets.

"We never go to the theatre or the cinema, but I think that's a good idea. We'll send what we can to the fund, Lydia."

"It's not enough Dikran. Think how we felt and what we needed after we were attacked by Talat Pasha. Money will help, of course, but we need to do more."

The next morning, they noticed that the speech was reported in the daily newspapers as Baldwin's appeal to the conscience of the British people. The journalists commented that his summary of the situation was eloquent and quoted from his speech: "Thousands of men, women and children, despoiled of their goods, driven from their homes, are seeking asylum and sanctuary on our doorsteps, a hiding place from the wind and a covert from the tempest."

Lydia learned what more she could do in conversation with Eva later that day. Eva and Raffi had met with Klaus and Gretel Krasnor and had news. The Krasnors were members of the British Jewish Refugee Committee, an organization that was working with Quaker community leaders and some other advocacy groups to pressure the British Government to facilitate ways of saving Jewish families from the Nazis. The events of Kristallnacht had provided the impetus for the government to agree, but only for children, not their parents.

"All children?" asked Lydia. "Babies?"

"Not babies," Eva responded. "Only children between two and seventeen years. The Krasnors, along with the other advocates, got the government to agree to a rescue mission. They said they'd allow up to one hundred thousand child refugees to come here. But not forever, mind you, only until they can be reunited with their parents. Let me get us some more tea."

"Thanks. But where will the children go—who will look after them? How will they prevent the children from being abused? I remember how difficult it was for me to be moved among families. Before the orphanages, I was bought and sold like cattle. Same with so many others. We were all so scared and so lonely. So hungry. We missed our families more than you'd ever imagine. Oh Eva, I wouldn't want that for anyone's children. What can we do? How can we help?"

"Funny you should ask." Eva smiled at Lydia. "They're looking for sponsors who will provide foster homes. They'll never get enough for all the children, and some will have to live in hostels or boarding schools, but... what do you think? Would you be willing to sponsor a child? No, don't answer right away. Think about it and talk to Dikran. Maybe you should also make sure your children are okay with having another child move in. After, we'll talk to the Krasnors."

Lydia, looking much less distressed than she had the previous minute, smiled, and said, "God is good—he has answered my prayers. We will help these children."

* * *

"Can we get a boy my age?" asked Leon, when Dikran and Lydia discussed fostering a child refugee from Germany with the family after dinner.

"No way," Miriam said emphatically. "I want a girl."

Dikran and Lydia looked at each other. The same idea occurred to them both. It would be a challenge. The house was not that large, but the possibility of caring for two children was immensely pleasing. They would manage, they decided.

* * *

The Krasnors identified a sibling pair who needed foster care. Ten-year-old Ben Rothman and his five-year-old sister, Bayla, were the children of a Jewish butcher. They had grown up in a small village where everyone knew everyone else, and everyone looked out for everyone else. It was an ideal childhood until Hitler came to power.

As Hitler's antisemitic sentiments spread to the village, attitudes toward the Rothman family changed. Children who had been friends with Ben and Bayla rejected them. Some spat at them and called them derogatory names. The hostility to the children increased dramatically after some teenagers in the village joined the Hitler Youth. Karl, a seventeen-year-old, stopped Ben one day as Ben was going home from school and beat him with a stick. Two days later, the Rothman butcher shop was vandalized.

The Rothmans knew they must let their children go to safety as soon as possible. They had heard of the British rescue plan—the kindertransport. Assuring the children they would see them again soon, and impressing upon them the need to be good, they asked Ben to care for Bayla and then took them to the train station. The last they saw of them was as they boarded the train full of children who were on their way to freedom in England.

Watching their parents become smaller and smaller as the train sped up and moved away from the platform, Bayla started to cry. Ben reached into his bag and handed her a biscuit from the snacks their mother had given him for the trip. It did little to calm her. He felt helpless and somewhat angry with the task of caring for his sister. He knew little more than she did about why they had been put on this train without their parents. Neither knew where they were going. Ben tried hard to be brave. He had to be. He had promised his mother. The train sped up and soon neither the platform nor the perimeter of the station were visible. A chorus of sobs filled the carriage.

28

It was a cold, damp morning in early December of 1938 when Lydia and Dikran watched anxiously as the children disembarked from the train. Lydia noticed that each of the children had a label pinned on their coat. The child's name, age, and sponsor's name were clearly written on the label. Lydia was pleased to see that every child's label listed a sponsor.

Lydia found out later that only the children who had already been assigned to sponsor families were on the train into London. She was dismayed to learn that the rest went to camps until boarding schools, hostels, or families could be found for them. She was even more concerned when she heard that those over the age of fourteen who did not have sponsor families were required to undergo a short course of training and then take a job, either in agriculture or as a domestic. Her biggest fear was that some would be mistreated or suffer the sort of sexual abuse she had.

Lydia became increasingly apprehensive as the children passed by her. She was shocked at how young some of them looked, but not at all surprised at how frightened they all looked. Seeing them, she was flooded with memories of how anxious she had felt when her mother sold her to a stranger who then sent her off with the Aydin family. She recalled the fear on the faces of the children who arrived at the orphanages in Aleppo. She wondered for what seemed like the millionth time what had happened to her younger brother. Dear little Luke, as she remembered him. Had he been terrified? Was he with a family? Was he killed? Clutching Dikran's hand, Lydia forced herself to block the thoughts of the past and concentrate on the children getting off the train.

Among the last to disembark, she noticed a boy who looked a little shorter than Leon, with his arm protectively around a younger girl. Both children had dark curly hair like that of Leon and Miriam, but shorter. The girl's eyes were red, and her cheeks were tear stained. She was leaning against the boy and clutching a rag doll close to her chest. The boy was holding a canvas bag.

"Willkommen," Lydia said, smiling at the pair, who she had accurately surmised were Ben and Bayla.

Dikran, who had also made a point of learning a few words of German from the Krasnors, greeted the children with "Hallo, wie geht's?"

It was a Friday, so Leon and Miriam were able to spend all of the next two days with Ben and Bayla and help them get adjusted. Leon, who would share his room with Ben, had voluntarily set aside some toys for Ben, and had identified some books he thought he might use to teach Ben a few words of English. Miriam was not pleased to be sharing her room. She had to be persuaded to set aside some toys and reluctantly agreed to do so only after Dikran insisted. But once the Vartounian children met the newcomers, they were full of empathy, and both behaved in the most welcoming and affectionate way they could.

"What about school for Ben and Bayla?" Leon asked. "What if the other kids are mean, like they have been to me? I don't want Ben to be hurt."

"I think it will be okay," replied Lydia. "I've talked to the teachers, and they've promised to explain the situation to the rest of the class and make sure Ben and little Bayla aren't bullied. I'll go with you to school on Monday morning and introduce Bayla and Ben to the head teacher."

Ben and Bayla were not the only "kinder" at school on Monday. Four other children had been sponsored by families in the area. The six emigrees were happy to be together, but the teachers wanted them to be accepted by, and part of, the larger group, rather than a clique unto themselves. The head teacher, Mrs. Massey, called the school together in the gym that morning to explain. Miriam felt very important when she and Leon were introduced as family for Bayla and Ben. They stood on the stage with the other children, feeling protective of their guests.

Lydia had talked to Mrs. Massey about her fears for the children, and Leon's experiences with bullies. Drawing on her experiences at the orphanage, and on her awareness of what would have helped her, she had suggested some role-taking exercises to help the British children understand the anxiety the newcomers would be feeling, especially with the language barrier. She also suggested that Mrs. Massey ask for volunteer "buddies" for each child to help them socially and with the language. Mrs. Massey was pleased with Lydia's suggestions and acted on them. They helped.

Lydia's suggestions to Dikran about Christmas were less well received. Lydia wanted to have a traditional family Christmas with attendance at St. Sarkis and the singing of Christmas Carols at home. Over the past year, she had been teaching Leon to play the piano, and he was ready to play a simple carol. She was both upset and embarrassed when Dikran reminded her that Ben and Bayla were Jewish and should not be expected to participate in Christian activities.

"What'll we do?" she asked Dikran. "We have to go to church, and I want Leon and Miri to enjoy their Christmas, as usual. But we can't just leave Ben and Bayla on their own. Surely it wouldn't hurt them to be part of our Christmas?"

"I understand, Lydia, and I have been thinking about it. I have an idea, and to be honest, I asked Raffi to check it out with the Krasnors, and they agreed it would be good."

"So, what is it?"

"We have both Christmas and Hanukkah. It'll be good for all four of them to learn about different religions, and the Krasnors thought that celebrating Hanukkah would really help Ben and Bayla adapt. Ben is old enough to help with the celebrations."

"I love the idea," Lydia replied at once, "but I know nothing about Hanukkah—what is it and what would we have to do? We can't really ask Ben yet. He doesn't have enough English to explain, and we don't have enough German. I'll talk to the Krasnors, and maybe I could ask at a synagogue; there's one close by I think."

Lydia learned that both the Christmas and Hanukkah celebrations commemorate a miracle so it may be possible for the family to hold both without spoiling either. Lydia had been concerned that it could be a sin for her family to observe Hannukah, but the more she learned about Hanukkah, the better she felt. Prior to making a final decision, she spoke to her priest. He assured her that it would be acceptable to celebrate both. She was relieved. Learning as much as she could about how Hannukah was celebrated, she set about preparations.

One of Lydia's concerns had been around gift-giving. Miriam and Leon would be expecting Christmas gifts, as usual. She did not want Ben and Bayla to be left out. It was with great relief and joy that she found that both celebrations involved giving children presents. Jewish children, she found out, often received chocolate coins wrapped in gold foil. When she located some for sale, she bought enough for all four children. When she bought books and jigsaws puzzles for Leon and Miriam, she bought copies of the A.A. Milne books and a puzzle for Ben, and a book and a teddy bear for Bayla.

Both celebrations also involved reading of particular scriptures. She decided she would get Ben and Leon to do the readings. Both celebrations also took place in December, but where Christmas was mostly over two days, Hanukkah was over eight. The main difference seemed to be the lighting of the menorah—an unadorned candelabra with nine branches. Lydia obtained a menorah through the Krasnors. Bayla and Ben could take turns lighting a candle each night until all eight were lit. There was one other thing she found out that she would have to do to help the children feel welcome and comfortable in their foreign environment. She would have to learn how to make latkes—a treat associated with Hanukkah.

For the Vartounian family, it turned out to be their best family December ever. And by the end of the month, the Bees, as Dikran referred to Ben and Bayla, were on their way to adapting to life in England.

They had excelled at learning to speak and understand English; they had adapted to the mix of Armenian and British foods, and they were playing with Leon and Miriam. Lydia encouraged them to write a long letter home to their parents. Ben wrote the letter, and Bayla drew some pictures. Lydia felt more relaxed. Her prayers on New Year's Eve were full of gratitude to God. She looked forward to a better year. Nineteen thirty-nine was just a few hours away.

29

Throughout January, it seemed like Lydia's conviction that 1939 would be a good year would be realized. Early in the month, to Lydia's relief, the Bees received a long letter from their parents. Included in the envelope was a separate letter thanking Dikran and Lydia for taking good care of the children. Lydia gave thanks to God that the Rothmans were still alive. She hoped for their sake that Ben and Bayla would be reunited with them in the coming months.

One evening in mid-February, over dinner, Dikran proudly informed the family that he would be promoted to the position of Inspector at the beginning of March. Lydia was pleased with the recognition and for the additional salary that came with the position. It would be helpful for Lydia's household budgeting. Dikran was relieved that he would no longer have to drive the trams in the fogs, which seemed to get worse each year. By April, there was a more compelling reason to be glad Dikran had been promoted.

In response to fears raised by Hitler's March occupation of Czechoslovakia and his seeming unlimited territorial ambitions, Britain introduced peacetime conscription. As an Inspector, Dikran was excused. If, as they thought unlikely, war broke out, Dikran would not have to join the military. Dikran had mixed feelings about this, but Lydia was unambiguously grateful to God that her husband would be spared the horrors of war if indeed it happened. She found it hard to accept the possibility of another war.

She tried to put thoughts of war aside by working in the garden. April flowers were up, and it was time to plant more herbs and vegetables. She sang hymns as she weeded, sowed, and planted. When she was feeling anxious, she hummed the "Ode to Joy." It was as calming as it had been when she was a child.

Nights were different. The more talk there was of Hitler and war, the more intense her flashbacks and nightmares. She wrote to Sarah of her fears, and she talked extensively with Eva. She prayed for peace. It all helped, but only a little. Dikran was becoming increasingly frustrated with his inability to comfort her. Waking to the sound of her screaming and the feel of the sweat dripping off her body several nights during the week was exhausting.

At Dikran's suggestion, Lydia made an appointment with the priest. For the first time, she told someone everything that had happened to her from the time the soldiers came to her home in Zeitun to her marriage to Dikran. In doing so, she realized she had been carrying an enormous burden of guilt. She felt guilty about what happened to her and the loss of her family, believing that she must have been responsible. And she felt guilty that she was not more grateful to God for Mrs. Sarkissian, the orphanage, her friends, her husband, and her children.

The priest was effective in helping her lessen the guilt. But both realized she had a long way to go. The healing would take time and conscious effort. He was unable to console her angst over the fate of her parents and younger brother. This unknown continued to haunt her daily. She agreed to talk with the priest again, and perhaps regularly. Ensuing events interfered.

Talk of war intensified through the summer. Lydia recalled being a small child sitting in the kitchen in Zeitun, listening to her parents talk about the possibility of war. She now wondered if they had known there was a possibility that Talat Pasha would invade. Would it have occurred to any of them that there would be a systematic effort to destroy the Armenian race? Could her Aunt Ruth have thought it possible that she would not be safe washing her clothes?

She realized Ben was about the same age she was that day her world turned upside down. She realized baby Ani would now be a young woman, perhaps a mother. It seemed impossible. Lydia tried to quiet the thoughts that spun repeatedly through her mind by taking the four children on picnics, to the zoo, to the park. She dug and weeded in her garden until she was exhausted. But the thoughts would not be quelled. The distraction, when it came, was worse.

"Lydia," Dikran said, after the children had gone to bed. "You're not going to be able to take the children to the park tomorrow. I'm not sure if you heard the news or checked the papers, but we are all to be fitted with gas masks, and tomorrow is our day to get them."

"What are you talking about, Dikran? I don't understand. Why do we need gas masks? Is the fog getting worse?"

Dikran smiled and then explained. "It's all this talk of war. Apparently, the government's scared the Nazis will drop poison gas bombs on us if there is a war. I don't think there will be, but I guess Mr. Chamberlain wants to be careful. He's probably remembering the first war when a lot of people were killed by chlorine gas or mustard gas or something like that. Anyway, tomorrow we all have to go get our masks."

"Even the children?" Lydia asked, aghast at the idea.

After waiting in line for what seemed like hours, it was finally their turn. Bayla was the first to be fitted. Because she was still only five years old, she was fitted with what was called a Mickey Mouse mask. The intent was for it to resemble the lovable Disney creature and so be less frightening for children aged two to five. But at the first sight of its bright red and blue rubber, huge ears, and weird eyes, Bayla had hysterics.

Miriam found it funny until it was her turn to be fitted with an ugly black rubber mask that was too tight on her face and smelled bad. The boys tried to be brave when they were fitted, but they both found it hard to breathe with the masks on and the smell, Leon complained, made him feel sick. The masks were packaged in cardboard boxes and the family was admonished to always keep them with them. It was emphasized to Dikran and Lydia that if caught without their masks, there would be fines to pay.

"But what about when the children go to school?" Lydia asked the government representative who was fitting them.

"They must take their masks with them." was the curt response. "Didn't you understand what I said? Masks must be carried with you at all times. No exceptions. Is that clear?"

The children hated having to carry the masks to school. What turned out to be worse was that the teachers, who had been especially trained to do so, held regular mask drills. Lydia loathed the thought of all those children sitting at their desks wearing the ugly rubber masks, looking like monsters, she thought.

The children hated it even more. Especially Miriam. In her class of forty children, Miriam was the first to find a way to stop hating the mask drills. She discovered she could make what she had learned were rude noises by blowing out through the rubber. The first time she did it, the teacher looked askance, assuming someone needed the toilet. At recess that day, Miriam told her peers how to make the noise. The next time there was a mask drill in their class, Miriam and all the other children blew raspberries.

Telling the boys later that evening, Miriam, giggling uncontrollably, explained it as a fart-fest. Lydia, who overheard, was horrified.

It started like most Sundays. A leisurely breakfast followed by church for the Vartounians, and a neighbour teenager coming in to stay with Bayla and Ben. As she was pinning on her best hat, Lydia noticed that the blue tattoos on her chin had faded considerably. She thought about all the times the children had asked her about them, and how impossible it was to talk about them.

"Where are those Bees?" asked Dikran as he was getting ready. "Jane will be here soon."

"Buzzzzzz" came the reply, as had become a family game over the past month with Ben and Bayla flapping their arms pretending to be bumble bees.

"Thanks Jane," said Lydia, as they were leaving. "We'll be back around eleven. You Bees be good." She hugged Ben and Bayla.

"Buzz," they said in response. With each carrying their gas mask, the family left.

Their world changed when they got home. Lydia made coffee while Dikran put the radio on the BBC. The usual Sunday programming they listened to was pre-empted by a statement from the Prime Minister. They sat side by side on the sofa to listen. What they heard was chilling. Neville Chamberlain announced Britain was now officially at war with Germany.

They sat staring at the radio in shock as they listened to his full five-minute statement. Chamberlain explained that since Hitler had failed to respond to British demands to leave Poland, "This country is at war with Germany". He emphasized his regret that although he had tried everything he could to avert a war, he had failed to do so.

Dikran and Lydia barely heard the announcements that followed Chamberlain's statement. All places of entertainment were to close immediately, and people were encouraged to avoid being in crowds except for church. Lydia heard the word church and began to focus. The next information described details of air-raid warnings. It was emphasized that tube stations were not to be used as bomb shelters. The importance of maintaining blackouts was stressed.

"Dear God, what is happening?" Lydia asked Dikran, her voice trembling. Before he could answer, an air-raid siren sounded. The children rushed into the living room. They were terrified by the noise and did not know what it was. Just as Dikran was about to gather his family and seek shelter, the announcer on the radio reported that it was a false alarm. But the war had officially begun.

* * *

"Where's Essex, dad?" asked Leon at dinner a few nights later.

"I think it's around a hundred and sixty miles northeast. We can look at a map. But why are you asking?"

"Well, you know how we all have to be dark all the time now cos of this war. Our teacher was telling us that a lot of people and animals have been hurt cos of the dark. So, this farmer in Essex painted white stripes on his cows so they wouldn't get run over. For real, she said. I wanna see those cows. Could we?"

The other children giggled. "Striped cows! Zebra cows, skunk cows, tiger cows." The children encouraged each other to think of other striped animals and the laughter increased with each example provided.

"How about painting spots and having Dalmatian cows?" asked Dikran with a straight face.

"Oh I know," said Miriam. "How about let's paint stripes on the Bees—that'll keep them safe and they'll look like bees."

"What do you think?" Dikran turned to Lydia as he asked the question. "Do we have enough paint?"

Lydia looked around the table and noted that for the first time in as long as she could remember, everyone was laughing. She realized how little laughter there had been in her life. What a strange time to experience it, she thought.

Listening to the laughter, Lydia thought how her decision not to allow the children to evacuate was right. There had been a lot of pressure on parents of school-age children to remove them from London. They were told that it was a city at high risk of attack. They should move the children to more rural areas.

The children would be taken by train or shipped down the Thames, accompanied by teachers and volunteers. They would be safe then. The government had issued a leaflet which Dikran and Lydia had received. It described Operation Pied Piper and listed the items each child was required to pack in readiness for the evacuation: gas masks, a change of clothing, toiletries, and so forth. When Lydia saw the leaflet, she asked Dikran what Pied Piper meant. It was not a term or a name with which she was familiar.

"It's an odd name for the evacuation of our children if the intent is to keep them safe," Dikran explained. "It's an old folk tale. This town called Hamelin was being overrun by rats. The Pied Piper was a man who wore a coat of many colours—"

"Like Joseph?" Lydia interrupted.

"Sure. That's why he was called Pied. And he was a piper because he played a flute. Not an ordinary one, but a magic one. He lived in a town where there were a lot of rats. So, he was hired to play his flute in a way that the rats would follow him out of town. He did and it worked. They went behind him out of the city gates and I guess to their doom. Thing was that the town then didn't pay him like they said they were going to. So, he went after the children. He piped a tune that made all the town's children follow him out of the town and they all vanished."

"And that's what'll happen to ours if we let them go, Dikran. I will never let any of them go. I will never forget how I felt when I was sent away from my mother. And the Bees—they have just started getting comfortable with us and their parents know where to write them letters, and oh, I cannot imagine letting any of them go anywhere. What a terrible thought. No, no, absolutely not. We will do our best to protect all four of them here. Nothing will break this family apart. I will never let my children go away from me."

"So, can we go see the cows?" Leon's question brought Lydia back to the present. She got up from the dinner table.

"Speaking of paint and the dark, I'd better get our windows done before we get in trouble." Lydia left to shut out the light with the heavy black drapes she had sewn. As she pulled them across, she realized she would again have to dust them. It was frustrating that the government officials had ordered no washing of blackout curtains. They said that once washed, light might escape the material. She hated the dust. She hated that not only did the curtains keep light out, but they also prevented air from coming in. But most of all, she hated them because of the reason they were there.

* * *

The blackouts had been in effect for only a few weeks. So far, the family had been little inconvenienced by them. The children were home from school long before sunset. It would be different as winter approached and the days grew shorter. Lydia was concerned.

Dikran had a meeting after work one night and came home well after dark. He had described how bewildering the experience was. The white paint around the doors of the tube trains and along the curbs was a help, but far from sufficient to feel confident where one was stepping, he had explained. Once the sun went down, everywhere was plunged into darkness. Streetlights were switched off, car lights were masked, and no buildings leaked any light at all. Maybe it would confuse the enemy, Dikran had said, but it may be confusing the citizens more.

"I could never see more than three feet in front of me," he had said in conclusion. "I walked with my arms outstretched like a robot, praying I wouldn't walk into a telephone booth, or building, or worse, into the road. It was awful."

31

By January of 1940, the Vartounians, like most of the population of Britain, had resigned themselves to the fact that Hitler had to be stopped by force, and that the blackouts were essential. What Lydia had a harder time accepting were the increasingly long queues for food. She had registered with her favourite shops as the government had required, and she was careful using the coupons in her ration book. But each day when she went shopping for groceries for dinner, it took much longer for her to purchase less for the days' meals.

With four children in the household, she could access milk and eggs, but meat, canned, and baked goods, were in short supply. Bacon, butter, and sugar were the first foods to be rationed. The Vartounians didn't eat bacon, but the lack of butter and sugar curtailed Lydia's cooking options. Many days, by the time she reached the front of the line, not only butter and sugar, but other items she needed would no longer be available.

At least, she thought, I do not have to show my children how to pick seeds from manure the way Anoush taught me. When Miriam complained about a meal, she was tempted to tell her that for many days, when she was a child, she had lived on grasses and seeds while being marched through the desert. But as always, she could not, or would not, talk about her experiences.

She did not want her children to know how debased she had been. She did not want to think about it. But too often, she would see her past as though it was a terrible movie that she could not stop watching. The movie just kept playing, over and over and over again. She would pray, asking God what he was punishing her for. She would beg for forgiveness. Then she would feel guilty and thank God for providing enough for her husband, her children, and the children they were caring for. But her past haunted her always.

Today had been particularly difficult. It was cold, rainy, and foggy, and she had got little sleep the night before. The children had been late leaving for school because Bayla had misplaced her gas mask. In turn, Lydia was late getting to the shops. Despite the gum boots and umbrellas, Lydia was soaked by the time she arrived at the shops. The line outside the butcher was the longest she had ever seen. After standing in the rain and fog for over an hour, she reached the front of the line only to find there was no meat left. There was only a hambone.

She found some tinned meat and tinned beans at the grocer, and one loaf of bread at the bakery. It had taken most of the day to purchase these few items. Now she had to figure out how to make an appetizing dinner with them that evening. She was frustrated and exhausted by the time she got home and try as she might to tell herself it wasn't that bad, it felt that bad.

She had barely removed her sopping wet coat when the children came home from school. The sun was already setting, so she asked Leon to help getting the blackout curtains drawn and then asked them to sit quietly with their books until their father was home and dinner was ready. She hoped she would feel more relaxed once her family was altogether and everyone had eaten. It did not turn out that way.

No one complained about the food. Lydia had created a reasonable meal by frying the meat in olive oil with some dried herbs and spices she had. She had a little rice left, which she steamed. She added the beans and sliced the bread.

"Pass the bread, please." Dikran was hungry.

Lydia passed the plate to Dikran. "Sorry, there's no butter. Again."

Dikran took a bite. "It's good without. Fresh."

Leon took a piece. "We don't need butter."

"I like it better with butter," said Miriam, and she made a sour face. But she took a piece and ate it quickly. Lydia again was tempted to tell the ungrateful child about eating grass and picking seeds from manure. They all ate hungrily in silence for a few moments. The mood at the table changed after Dikran asked each of the children what they had learned at school that day.

Bayla wanted to go first. She talked about a drill the children had to do with their gas masks. They all knew the drill, she said. "First you take it out of the box, then you put it on your face, then you make sure it's on okay, and then you breathe." But, she said the children were very naughty that morning and not taking the drill seriously. "My friend Lisa pretended she didn't know how to put the mask on and put it on backwards. A boy put his on the top of his head. Then a lot of the children started making rude noises with them, you know, like Miri does. It was really funny." She started giggling, remembering it. The teacher, she said, got quite cross with them.

Ben said he had learned more about the Regent's Park Zoo. "My teacher told us that the zoo had expected there was gonna be a war, so even before it started, they had moved some animals to some other place. I can't remember where, but something like Whipster."

"Probably Whipsnade Wild Animal Park. It's outside London, so they probably thought it would be safer." Dikran suggested.

"That's it." Ben replied.

"Which animals did they move?" Leon asked.

"They moved some giant pandas, orangutans, chimpanzees, elephants, and um, oh, I remember an ostrich." Ben was marking off the animals on the fingers of his left hand.

"Sounds like Noah loading up the ark." Lydia commented, starting to relax and enjoy the children's accounts.

Ben went on to tell the family that the zoo had also killed some of the poisonous creatures so they wouldn't get loose in London and hurt people if the zoo was bombed. Miriam thought that was funny.

"I wanna go next." Miriam said impatiently.

"Okay with me, my day was kinda boring." Leon sat back to wait his turn.

Miriam explained that first thing in the morning, the class had welcomed back two children who had been evacuated at the start of the war. They had gone to stay with their grandparents in Dorset. But they got bored, and their parents missed them, so they came home.

"After that," Miriam continued, "we went round the class, and we were all supposed to talk about our family, and why family is important." Lydia tensed, sensing what might be coming.

"That's nice, Miri," she said, hoping it would forestall anything further. It did not.

"It was awful. Everyone 'cept me talked about their aunties, and uncles, and cousins, and grandparents, though some said theirs was dead. And I asked teacher what's a cousin and all the others laughed at me. What is a cousin anyway, and why don't we have grandparents and aunties and uncles? When I said I don't have any, teacher got angry and thought I was just being bad. The other kids said that's dumb. Everyone has aunties and uncles and grandparents. Why can't you talk about yours? Why don't we mummy? Why don't you tell me? Where're my grandparents? Why don't I have all the family that all the other children have? It's not fair." She started to cry.

Lydia started to shake. Dikran noticed and quietly put his hand on her knee to calm her.

"Miriam," Lydia said. The frustrations of the day surged. She was unable to control the anger in her voice. "Can't you ever let it be? Why are you always the problem in this family? You have two parents, and a brother, and the Bees. That's your family. It should be enough. Nothing is ever enough for you, Miriam, is it?"

Both Miriam and Bayla burst into tears at the rare outburst.

"Lydia," Dikran said, "That's enough. This is not like you. You must have had a very bad day."

"I did, I'm sorry." Tears were running down Lydia's face. The children stared at her. They were upset and shocked. The stunned silence at the table was shattered by the piercing shriek of an air-raid siren.

"Under the table," Dikran commanded. The family huddled together under the dining table. Miriam made a point of lying close to Lydia with her arm tightly round her.

32

"We have to get a proper shelter," Lydia said as the family clung to each other and prayed that they would be spared the bombing. "I know none of us wants to go back to the shelter in the tube station, but we are not safe like this."

The first time they sheltered in an underground station—they were now legitimate shelters—they almost enjoyed the experience. People were chatting and saying things like "It's very blitzy, isn't it?" Dikran thought it sounded like people discussing the weather at the local pub. The children thought it was very funny. "Are you blitzy, Bayla?" Miriam giggled.

Lydia was too focused on the safety of the children to notice. A local librarian had bought in some books for the children to read, and a violinist was playing some soothing music. It was stuffy and crowded, but morale stayed high. The next time was entirely different.

The Vartounian family were among the last to arrive at the shelter. There was a long queue to get in and tempers were getting shorter with each passing moment. By the time they got in, the shelter was crowded, noisy, and smelly. Some people were arguing over space, a couple of men were fighting, babies were crying, and some children had wet themselves.

"You'd think there would be toilets somewhere," Lydia had said, exasperated. They managed to squeeze themselves into a small space and sat on the floor to await the all-clear. Almost as soon as they sat down, some people who were beside them started loudly expressing antisemitic attitudes.

"I don't know why these Jews have to hog all the space in the shelters," said a middle-aged woman.

"I know," replied the man with her, "it's bloody awful. Dunno who they think they are. Feckin Jews!"

Ben put his arm protectively around Bayla.

Dikran put his hand on Lydia's arm and suggested it would be best for them to say nothing. He wished he were home, quietly reading the newspaper.

"We're not Jews, are we mummy?" Miriam asked.

"No silly," replied Leon, "we're Christian Armenians, but the Bees are Jewish. Why are these people so mean, dad?" he asked.

The middle-aged woman turned to Lydia. "Why doncha take your damn kids—so many of them you must breed like a cow—just get outta here. We don't want folks like you."

The all-clear sounded and the family left quickly. They were shaken by the experience. Dikran tried to explain to the children that when afraid, people say and do things that are inappropriate. It did not quiet Ben and Bayla.

"Do you think we can go home to our real parents now?" Ben asked. Bayla was quietly crying.

Dikran explained that it would not be safe. They might be killed if they tried. Lydia tried to comfort the Bees by hugging each of them and saying how much they would be missed. She also told them what she had kept from them previously. That their parents had written and asked if they could stay longer in London because they believed no Jews were safe in Germany. It was a difficult conversation.

After that experience, the family decided they would not go back to a communal shelter. But it soon became clear that something more than the dining table was needed to keep them safe.

In late August, central London was bombed for the first time. It was eventually reported that the bombing was in error. The Luftwaffe had been aiming for military targets on the outskirts of the city, but somehow ended up dropping their bombs on central London. The bombs devastated the area between St. Paul's Cathedral and the Guildhall. They also destroyed homes. And civilians were killed. Seeing the photos of the devastation beneath the headlines in the papers was frightening. A proper bomb shelter became essential.

Lydia and Dikran researched options and decided on an Anderson Shelter. They read that these shelters were easy to assemble, strong, and could house up to six people. Lydia also determined that the Vartounians qualified for a free one. They had a garden that would accommodate it, they were below the income cut-off required, and they had no appropriate room for protection within the house. Soon after Dikran applied, the six corrugated steel panels arrived. He was informed that he was expected to have it erected within two weeks.

The shelter was intended to be installed a yard below the ground, so the first task was to dig a hole in the garden big enough for it to be semi-buried. Dikran asked the boys to help him dig the hole.

"How big does it need to be?" asked Leon.

"Well," Dikran replied, "the shelter is six and a half feet long and four and a half feet wide, so a bit bigger than that. I've an idea. Let's give it a name." He thought for a few seconds. "I know. What do you think of Andromeda?"

"Andy for short?" asked Ben. "Why Andromeda?"

"Sure, Andy it is. Andromeda is a Greek name that means protector of mankind. Andy will be our protector. Okay boys, let's get digging."

"Won't mum be upset that we've dug up her rhubarb?"

"I thought of that, Leon," Dikran responded, "but you know what we can do? We'll have to put soil on top of Andy once we get him built and buried, so why don't we plant some veges on his head—sort of like hair?"

Over the next ten days, Dikran assembled, buried, and furnished the shelter. It was small, dark, and dank. But it was private, quiet, and safe. With help from the boys, Dikran built three sets of bunk beds which barely fit. The girls would share a bunk, as would the boys, and Dikran and Lydia. A bucket in the corner was the best they could do for a toilet. Dikran discussed plantings with Lydia. They decided they would plant a few flowers to keep their spirits up. But they would use most of the space for vegetables. They planned to plant rhubarb, squash, cauliflower, and runner beans. Even though it was late in the season, Miriam made a compelling argument for strawberries. They were added. Miriam enjoyed planting them herself. She also planned to eat them herself.

The government had recommended that the shelters be used regularly as a place to sleep. But the Vartounians decided Andy was too dank and crowded for regular use. They would go in only when the air-raid siren sounded. In practice, this turned out to mean most nights in the shelter. Dikran and the children got used to sleeping there. Lydia was too tense to sleep, too concerned about their safety. She coped by taking some needlework or crochet with her. She usually had to unpick what she had done in the shelter because, with only candlelight, it was too dark to see the stitches, but the effort kept her from panicking.

Over the next few months, they realized that Andy, as they routinely referred to the shelter, was living up to his name. They felt protected, albeit uncomfortable, when in him. The Bees wrote a long letter to their parents about Andy. Bayla drew a picture of him, which they put inside the letter. Lydia added a note, reassuring the Rothmans that the children were doing well and were safe. She wished she believed that. The truth was, she was afraid for them.

There were many nights that the children and Lydia were in the shelter without Dikran. Since the start of the so-called Blitz in September, Dikran was often out at night fire-watching. Lydia worried constantly about his safety. She prayed endlessly that God would protect him. She believed her prayers were answered on the night of October fourteenth when he came home very late, shaking and ashen.

He collapsed into a chair and asked for a moment before talking. She made him some tea.

"Lydia, tonight I saw hell," he started after taking a couple of gulps of the hot sweet tea. "I was doing a routine inspection on the number eighty-eight bus. It was difficult with the blackouts, but I had a good chat with the driver. Everything seemed okay, so I got off. A couple minutes later, I heard the most enormous explosion of my life—a sound I never want to hear again."

"A bomb?" asked Lydia.

"Not just any bomb. This bomb went right through the road and exploded in the Balham Tube Station. The ground shook, and I saw that it'd made the most enormous crater—right in front of me Lydia— and—." His voice faltered. He stopped and drank some more of the tea. Lydia sat quietly beside him.

"The bus, Lydia, the bus I had been on just a few minutes earlier, fell right into the crater with all the people on it and Pete, the driver. It was just so horrible, horrible. It wasn't Pete's fault. What could he do? He's driving in a blackout and suddenly there's this hole in the road in front of him. I don't even know if he could have seen it. I heard people screaming, I heard gushing water, and there was a terrible smell of burning and sewage. It sounded like the pipes had just exploded. Then I saw people scrambling out, many of them bleeding. Some of them were soaked. All of them...." He could not continue.

"Shush now, Dikran, you don't have to say anything more now. Maybe it's not as bad as you think. Maybe God was there and looking out for all those people. I will pray for them. And God answers my prayers. He saved you. Come get some sleep."

Getting up the next morning after a sleepless night, Dikran scoured the newspapers for details. There were no reports of the bombing and devastation in any of the London papers or on the radio. He asked others about it at work. No one other than he had been in the area, so no one had seen or heard of it. He wondered if the whole thing was some awful nightmare. But over the next ten days, news emerged.

Dikran learned that the government had been trying to keep the incident quiet and so had not allowed the newspapers to publish the story. They did not want people to be afraid of using the air-raid shelters in the tube stations. To his horror, Dikran learned that along with the physical devastation to the tramlines, the water mains, and the sewage pipes, almost seventy people had been killed. To his relief, he learned that many more had escaped and survived, the bus driver, Pete, and all his passengers among them.

Lydia was most relieved that the children did not hear about the tube station bombing. She could, however, do little to protect them from the endless sounds of the air-raid sirens that they hated so much. And she could do little to protect them from the nightly attacks on the city. Now, well into winter, they had to spend every night in Andy. Each night at dusk, the sirens would alert them to the need to take shelter. The all-clear would not sound until daybreak the next morning. Some nights it was relatively quiet, and they could get some sleep. Others they could hear bombs. The children were getting increasingly afraid. The Bees begged to be able to go home.

Occasionally, they would stop and admire a star-filled sky before climbing into the shelter, but such nights were rare. It seemed like the raids were going on forever. Every night, there were sirens and the explosions when bombs dropped or when a plane was hit. The shaking ground. The thump thump thump of falling shrapnel. They would stay in Andy, praying for safety. Lydia would try to get them to sing, although she avoided most of her favourite hymns out of respect for the Bees' religion.

Some nights, Lydia would tell the children stories. Her preference was to read Bible stories. But she settled on a series of bedtime stories for children that illustrated the values she associated with a good Christian life. Each story would teach children the benefits of being helpful, generous, well-mannered, and obedient. She realized as she read them that the Bees and Leon were already displaying these behaviours.

Miriam, however, was different. Miriam was having a more difficult time adjusting to life through the Blitz than the other children. Lydia was understanding and remained patient and supportive of her daughter. She was glad when Dikran was there. When he was with them, using only the candlelight in Andy, Dikran would read from *The House at Pooh Corner*, a book they all still loved. He would also play board games with the children while Lydia crocheted. She thanked God daily for Dikran, Andy, and the safety of all the children. She prayed they would continue to stay safe.

Lydia was particularly grateful that they did not need to go to the communal shelters. Not only had the antisemitic slurs upset her profoundly, but she heard from other women in the shops that conditions in the shelters had worsened. There were now thousands of people cramming into them every night. Long queues started long before they were open. The British Red Cross and the Salvation Army were trying to improve conditions in the shelters. Some now had stoves and they were working on the provision of toilets. But none, she knew, would afford the peace, comfort, and privacy of Andy.

Lydia was also grateful that Andy provided a diversion for the children during the days when they were not in school. Miriam would tend her strawberry patch, although it was months before she could expect any fruit. Bayla would look after the few winter flowers that survived. And Ben and Leon had decided to decorate Andy and were painting "Andromeda" in fancy lettering on one side where the shelter protruded above ground.

The vegetables on the top of the shelter had done well and were providing much needed nutrition for the family. Vegetables were not rationed. But there rarely were any available at the greengrocer shops. Lydia had vegetables growing in every available inch of their garden. She had been successful enough that she could also share some with their friends Eva and Raffi. Shortly before the outbreak of war, they had moved closer to Lydia and Dikran's new home.

Superficially, Lydia was coping well. But she was troubled by the growing anger she felt about her life. Each day, she felt more resentful of all the evils that had and continued to beset her. Each day she felt angrier that God would allow such. Each day, she wondered why God was punishing her. Each day, she prayed for forgiveness. Her inner turmoil was constant.

Despite her anger and despair, Lydia, with Dikran's help, gave all the children a pleasant experience through Hanukkah and Christmas. They put the menorah in Andy and hung paper chains the children had made from the bunk bed rails. On boxing day, she wrote a long letter to Sarah in which she expressed her feelings and stated her hope that as the year ended, the bombings would stop. Three days later, the worst bombing of the war occurred in London.

34

Dikran was on his way home when the first air-raid siren sounded. He went as fast as he could to get to Andy. It was difficult to hurry in the blackout, but he was confident he knew where he was and that he was closer to Andy than any other shelter. He also wanted to be with the family. Just as he approached the garden, he heard the whistling of the bombs. He realized that meant a bomb was within a few hundred yards. As he reached Andy, the sky turned orange. There were black clouds of smoke. He heard more whistling. The ground shook beneath him.

Slipping inside and slamming the door, Dikran was acutely aware that this was the second time he had narrowly escaped death. The bombing that night seemed to go on forever. The drone of the planes was endless. The whistling bombs, the thump of shrapnel, the smell of fire, and the shaking ground frightened them all.

"What's happening, Dikran?" Lydia's voice was trembling.

"Guess we'll find out in the morning." Dikran sounded tired and impatient. Bayla started to cry.

Around eleven, the all-clear sounded. They calmed but remained apprehensive. Dikran stepped outside Andy to see what was happening. He was horrified. It looked like the whole of London was on fire.

"Lydia," he said, going back into the shelter, "I'm going to help with the firefighting. I can't just stay here—looks like a firestorm out there. Take good care of the children." He left before she could object. Lydia had been afraid of something like this occurring since Dikran had joined the Auxiliary Fire Brigade the previous year.

Despite the darkness, it was obvious to Dikran that the damage to the city was extensive. From what he could see, the area around St. Paul's Cathedral was fully engulfed in flame. He headed in that direction. The scene and the efforts to extinguish the fires were beyond anything Dikran could have imagined. Thousands of incendiary bombs had been dropped. Extensive areas of the city were ablaze.

Dikran joined the hundreds of firefighters who were struggling to contain the flames. The firefighters were hampered by a strong wind that was fanning the flames and by a water main that had been ruptured by a bomb. This, together with their efforts to get water from other areas, caused a serious drop in water pressure. They then tried to get water from the river Thames. But the tide was low, causing their hoses to get clogged with mud. Despite the odds, most of the fires were extinguished by dawn.

At first light, the vast extent of the devastation was clear. Dikran thought that Prime Minister Churchill would be pleased that St. Paul's Cathedral had been saved. But several historic churches had been destroyed, and the entire area between the Cathedral and the Guildhall was devastated. Fires continued to burn. Worse, over two hundred fire-fighters had been injured and fourteen died. Dikran shuddered when he realized how close he had come to being one of them.

* * *

Lydia and the children were profoundly relieved when Dikran arrived home mid-morning. He looked exhausted and beaten. His skin was blackened by the smoke, and his clothes reeked of fire. He hugged each of his family.

"I'm okay," he told them. Once the children were out of hearing, he told Lydia of his third narrow escape.

"I was holding a hose, trying to get enough water on a church wall to save the church. Someone called out that they needed help with the hydrant. I was going to put the hose down and go help, but this young lad said he'd hold the hose while I went. I passed it to him without thinking. But almost immediately the wall that I, and then he, had been spraying, collapsed. The young lad was buried under it, along with another man who'd been there. We tried to dig them out. It was too late Lydia."

"It seems God has a purpose for you. He needs you on this earth, Dikran." Silently, Lydia once again thanked God for saving her husband. She held him until he stopped shaking.

Each of the children was affected by the night of bombing. Bayla cried more than she had before. Miriam was increasingly disobedient and rude. Leon, always an easy and compliant child, became aggressive. Ben became withdrawn. Lydia tried her best to comfort them, but she also was stressed, anxious, and short-tempered. She wondered if she was transmitting her emotions to the children. She had made a point of not sleeping the nights they were in Andy. It was the only way she could prevent the nightmares and the screams that so often accompanied them. But the lack of sleep had caught up with her. She hoped once school was back after the Christmas break, things would ease up. They didn't.

It was only two weeks after the dreadful night of bombs and fires, of terror and trauma, that Leon came home from school talking about a newspaper article he had read. He had seen the headlines at a shop and stopped to read the article.

"It's never gonna stop, is it?" he started. "I read today that another tube station was bombed, and more people killed. And killed horribly. It said that a bomb exploded where the escalator is—there were people sleeping there and there were some sleeping on the platforms—they were killed. The paper said that some were thrown in front of a train and got run over. We're all gonna get killed, aren't we? What's the point of going to school? We're just gonna die. And why are the Bees still here, anyway? Don't they have a home?"

Once again, Lydia wished she could talk to the children about her experiences in the desert. It would help them understand that extraordinary hardships could be overcome. But she couldn't. She wouldn't. She thought about how she had survived the horrors of the first world war, only to experience those of the second. How could she comfort Leon when she herself shared his despondency? If only they could all go to the zoo, have a picnic with Eva and Raffi and their children, she thought, do something normal. But the zoo had closed the previous year because of the war. And it had been years since she had even had lunch with Eva. There was only this horrible new normal.

* * *

Dikran's timing was perfect. Just as Lydia was wondering how to comfort Leon, Dikran walked in the door with the ultimate distraction. In his arms was a small bundle of golden fur.

"I was walking home when I heard an unusual sound—sort of a cry," Dikran explained. "I looked around and saw nothing. Then I heard it again, and I traced it to, of all things, a dustbin. I took the lid off and, saw this little puppy. Some awful person must have put him in there. What else could I do but rescue him?"

The children rushed over as Dikran put the pup down.

"He looks just like my teddy bear." Miriam squealed with delight. "We can keep him, right mummy? I'll look after him. I really will, I promise."

"So will I," added Leon, his bad temper replaced with a broad smile.

"Can we help too?" asked the Bees.

"I bet he's hungry" Lydia looked on the kitchen counter to see if there was food suitable for a dog.

"Looks like he's going to be one of our family now." Dikran was pleased with the reactions. "But he needs a name."

"Cuddles" suggested Bayla.

"No. Winnie!" Miriam said decisively.

"After Prime Minister Churchill?" Dikran asked her, teasingly.

"No, silly daddy. After Winne the..." she turned to the other children, grinning.

"Pooh!" they shouted in unison.

Winnie went to Miriam and licked her face appreciatively.

"Does Winnie need a gas mask?" asked Bayla. Dikran shook his head; the other children laughed.

"Well, Winnie, welcome to our home." Lydia was delighted, anticipating that the pup would be good for all of them.

35

Winnie's adoption improved things for the children. Petting him was calming, and his antics caused great amusement. Having him in Andy helped the children cope with the endless sound of the sirens and the bombs, as they focused on keeping Winnie calm. And once the Blitz ended, in May of 1941, there was no more time in the shelter. But daily life remained full of challenges for Lydia.

Rationing had increased to include clothing and soap. Lydia responded by spending more time altering the children's clothing so that something fit everyone, and by spending her evening darning Dikran's socks and sweaters. She had used most of their old linens to patch clothing, but she still had some lace that she had brought with her from Aleppo. She sewed pieces of lace over the worn patches in her dresses. As well as increased rationing, shortages and long queues were increasingly common.

Each morning, Lydia would take Winnie on his leash and her gas mask in its case in one hand, and her shopping bag in the other to the shops. As she walked, she hoped and prayed that she could find something to feed the family. What they had most often were vegetables from the garden. But that was not enough. All of them were losing weight. She was unconcerned for herself but did not like to see the children growing taller and skinnier. She was concerned that they were tired often and worried they would fall ill from poor nutrition. Feeding Winnie was a struggle as well. Fortunately, the butcher had become very fond of the dog and saved whatever few soup bones he had not sold to customers for Winnie.

Lydia spent her afternoons working in the garden and creating some kind of meal for dinner. Vegetable soup was the most frequent. In the evenings, after she cleared dinner and got the children to bed, she did her mending and, if time allowed, knitting. Not only was she always exhausted, but she noticed that she sometimes felt short of breath. It was worse on days that were damp and foggy, and when she was carrying a heavy shopping bag. Since the cessation of the air raids, she had been sleeping better and the nightmares were less frequent. It wasn't lack of sleep, she thought, that caused her difficulties. She wondered if she should see a doctor, but felt too busy and tired to do so.

Dikran was every bit as tired as Lydia. He was working overtime to raise extra cash for the family. He was also still volunteering as a firefighter. Most nights he got home after dark. Finding his way home every night in the blackouts was stressful and exhausting. He heard a car crash on more than one evening, and periodically, another pedestrian bumped into him. He had heard from his colleagues at work about the increase in crime that had accompanied the blackouts and was always worried about the family.

Dikran was particularly disturbed that there had been two murders of women in October of 1941 that had remained unsolved. One was a young woman, a nineteen-year-old clerk. The papers reported that she was known to frequently meet up with servicemen and engage in sexual behaviour with them. Dikran wondered if one of the men she met had killed her.

The other murder was of more concern to Dikran. A forty-eight-year-old widow had been found lying on her bed in her Regent's Park home with extensive and vicious injuries. She died in hospital. It made Dikran anxious. The blackout could provide cover for almost anything, he thought. He was fearful for Lydia. He hoped Winnie would turn into a good guard dog as well as their source of comfort and entertainment. He was glad that Winnie always accompanied Lydia on her shopping trips.

The children had their own concerns. Leon was nearing age fourteen, which meant he would finish school. He enjoyed learning and his academic performance was excellent. He did not want to stop his education and get a job, but he would have no choice. What he really wanted was to go to university.

Since they had adopted Winnie, Leon had become increasingly interested in animal welfare and had decided that he might like to become a vet. He also thought about becoming a doctor. One of his classmates had died from scarlet fever, and another from a traffic accident in the blackouts. He thought they both should have been saved.

Leon did not want to spend his life working in a factory or as a firefighter. But it seemed he would have to do so for a few years. In discussions with Dikran, he decided he would join the fire brigade next year when school was finished. Once the war was over and after he had saved some money, he planned to go to university.

Miriam's difficulties were the opposite of Leon's. She hated school. She did well academically, but she was always in trouble. Most recently, she'd been caught making faces at the teacher. "I have to write a hundred lines again tonight." She would often complain to Lydia about lines.

"What did you do now?

"Today I have to write 'I will not make faces at the teacher.' Last time I had to write 'I will not giggle in class.' Why don't they leave me alone? What's the point of these stupid lines?"

"You're lucky they just make you write lines and don't give you the strap, young lady." Lydia was not sympathetic.

"No, but last week, teacher hit my hand with a ruler, and yesterday I had to stand in the corner for ten minutes. It was awful."

"Well, Miri, maybe you should behave yourself sometimes."

Leon and Miriam were continuing to get along with the Bees, but there was also a growing sense among the family that it was time for the Bees to return home. The Bees were most eager to do so. They had adapted well to life in London and the use of English, but they missed their parents intensely. They had been receiving regular letters from their parents, but nothing had come for over three months. Lydia knew Berlin had been bombed. She prayed that the Rothman family was safe.

* * *

It seemed to Lydia that every year of her life since she was ten had been eventful. Nineteen forty-two was no exception. In January, she was diagnosed with asthma. Her doctor prescribed a variety of tablets, suppositories, and injections. They helped to some extent. They did not help enough when the air was full of smoke from coal fires and fog. On those days, Lydia struggled to breathe. She was looking forward to summer weather and the end of smoke and coal dust in the air.

Headlines in the papers in February gave Lydia more to worry about. Over a six-day period, four more women were murdered. Banner headlines reading "The Blackout Killer" were hard to avoid. The victims were a variety of ages, some younger than Lydia, some a few years older. Dikran had seen the headlines on his way home. He urged Lydia to be extra careful and never leave the house without Winnie. Lydia was relieved when, a few days after the grisly discoveries of the mutilated bodies, the papers reported that a suspect, Gordon Cummins, had been arrested. His trial in April resulted in a guilty verdict and a sentence of death by hanging.

Lydia wondered if the state killing of a murderer was an appropriate response. It did not seem very Christian. She then recalled how she had felt when she heard Talat Pasha had been killed. She discussed her mixed feelings with Dikran.

"I like to think that I am a pacifist and against capital punishment," he replied. "I wish I could believe in the teachings of the Sermon on the Mount in Matthew, but I can't believe Jesus meant it literally. Should we wait for God to mete punishment? I don't know Lydia. But I do know that I could not help feeling great relief when Cummins was executed."

Ben and Leon had seen the headlines and were full of questions. They were distracted, however, by the arrival of the American soldiers, or GIs, as they were called. Landing in Britain in 1942, the GIs brought with them a wide variety of treats and American culture. The children were thrilled with the sweets, the chewing gum, and the Coca Cola. The arrival of the GIs also distracted the Bees from worrying about the increasing of time since there had been a letter from their parents.

The children all soon learned to run up to the soldiers shouting, "Got any gum, chum?" Lydia allowed them to take part in this practice. She enjoyed seeing them being playful. She also noticed, to her surprise, that young women were eagerly accepting nylon stockings and cigarettes from the GIs. Lydia was glad that Miriam, at twelve, was still young enough to be happy with sweets—at least for a while. Miriam decided she would marry an American. "Then I can just drink Coca Cola and eat sweets and wear fancy nylon stockings," she explained.

Leon was puzzled by the Americans. His knowledge of American men came exclusively from the few films he had seen. "They're not as tall as I thought, dad," he said, "and they don't have those guns and hats I thought they all had."

Dikran was amused. "Did you think they were all cowboys, with big hats and guns strapped on their hips?"

Dikran realized his son was not alone in his thinking when he read in *The Times* newspaper a message to the public stating that the GIs were "friendly and simple" rather than "Hollywood stars or two-gun Texans with five-gallon hats." He read the message to Lydia and told her what Leon had said. Lydia was pleased to share a laugh with Dikran. Laughter had remained rare. That night, Lydia turned to Dikran. She lay contentedly in bed after they made love, appreciating that she could now enjoy sex with her husband.

The distraction afforded by the GIs was temporary. Early in the new year, twenty-three people were killed and many more were injured by shrapnel shells during a bombing raid on London.

"Will this never stop?" Lydia asked Dikran that evening. A few days later, she was devastated to learn that thirty-eight children and six of their teachers had been killed by a bomb in southeast London. She spent increasing amounts of time in prayer, pleading with God to make the bombing stop. She decided her prayers were answered and gave thanks to God when, over the next few months, there were no major raids on London. Spring turned into summer and every member of the family relaxed.

36

It was a warm and sunny day in June of 1944. Lydia's asthma was not bothering her, and she had spent an enjoyable afternoon weeding the garden and harvesting vegetables for dinner. Winnie had tried to help, but he and Lydia did not agree on what should be dug up. She took him for a walk before the children came home from school. She was feeling unusually relaxed, which she attributed to the peacefulness and the warmth of the sun. The nightly bombing raids, when they all huddled in Andy, seemed a distant past. Miriam's strawberries were growing on the roof now, along with some vegetables. Lydia had felt happy all day. But her contentment did not last. That night London, as it had three years earlier, came under heavy attack.

Lydia woke toward dawn to what sounded to her like a motorbike in poor condition, struggling up a steep hill. She heard a distant explosion.

"Dikran." She nudged him awake. "I think I heard another bomb dropping."

"No, Lydia. They stopped. Go back to sleep," he said, but then the air-raid siren sounded.

London once again had become the favourite target of the Luftwaffe. This time with newly developed flying bombs—unmanned aircraft carrying large explosive warheads. They were fired from Nazi occupied Europe. The bombs were soon nicknamed doodlebugs or buzz bombs based on the sound they made in flight.

Miriam liked the name and would draw her version of a doodlebug. Leon told her it looked like a fat beetle wearing trousers. Miriam giggled.

"Stop it," Lydia said. "This is no joking matter. If you want to draw a picture, draw something nice."

The doodlebug that woke Lydia that night in June was the first of thousands to drop on London over the next eight months. There were constant massive explosions day and night as the doodlebugs just kept coming. Air-raid sirens seemed endless. It was not unusual to hear multiple air-raid sirens in a day. One evening, over just a few hours, there were five separate air-raid warnings.

Lydia's nightmares became more frequent again. The children were increasingly upset, anxious, and difficult to calm, even with Winnie. Winnie himself needed calming. The constant sirens and explosions made him as anxious as the children. He would alternate between running in circles, barking, and cowering under the dining room table.

Andy was back in regular use. Lydia was glad she had kept the shelter clean and usable. But she despaired that they needed to use it again as they had during the Blitz. Lydia, the Bees, Miriam, and Winnie spent many uneasy hours together waiting for Dikran and Leon to come home. Dikran was again busy as a firewatcher, and Leon was appointed to a special fire prevention crew whose task was to watch over historic buildings. They were at home infrequently and for only short periods of time.

Lydia's anxiety was heightened by the frequent and loud roaring clatter of the doodlebugs. They had an unusual engine noise. Lydia's initial thought that she'd heard a struggling motorbike was consistent with how they were later described in the papers. When one ran out of fuel and was about to drop, the engine would sputter and stop. It would nose-dive and about ten seconds later, there would be an enormous explosion. Everyone learned quickly that when the sound of the doodlebug stopped, they had little time to take cover before it exploded on impact with the ground.

The doodlebugs caused extensive damage around London, including their neighbourhood. After one relatively close explosion, the windows of the Vartounian home were blown out. Dikran fixed them, but a few days later they were blown out again.

"Well Lydia," he said. "We're in good company. A chap at work was telling me that one of these wretched doodlebugs narrowly missed landing on Buckingham Palace. It missed, but it blew out some windows."

"God bless the King," Lydia responded, "and may God spare us all from anything worse than broken glass."

Their neighbours were not spared. One night in August, the sirens and then the sound of the doodlebug engine stopping sent the family to Andy seconds before the doodlebug exploded. It exploded across the street from their house. Huddled in Andy, they could feel the vibrations, they could smell the fire, they could hear glass breaking, and they realized the chaos that was unfolding. They heard ambulances, people calling out to each other, people screaming, babies crying, and dogs barking. Dikran, home that evening, stepped out to survey the extent of the damage.

Mortar dust and rubble filled his vision. He heard coughing and crying. He realized that at least three houses across the street were destroyed. Through the dust, he saw one of their neighbours, Janet Taylor, standing in the rubble. He called to her to come into Andy. He ran over and helped her across. Together, they stumbled across the street, avoiding shards of glass, broken bricks, and pieces of steel. In the few moments it took to get to Andy, they both were covered in dust. They coughed consistently. Janet was shaking uncontrollably and crying.

"My husband!" Janet cried. "Nigel's in there. The wall fell on him. I couldn't get to him. My baby's crib's buried under bricks and chunks of metal—she was sleeping there." She sobbed uncontrollably. "I don't know where my son is. He's only eight. Oh God...." She could talk no more. She collapsed onto the floor in a heap of despair. Winnie went over and tried to comfort her by licking her face.

"I'll make you some tea. You're in shock." said Lydia, helping Janet to a chair. "Come sit here. Miriam, please stay with Janet while I get the tea." As she made the tea, she reflected on how Janet had been among those who ignored her when she first moved in. It was only after Nigel had bumped into her in the fog that they had become acquainted. For a long time, Nigel had been friendly, but Janet had remained distant. Things changed when the war started. Janet and Nigel Taylor had become good neighbours.

"I'll go see if I can find your family," Dikran said. "Leon, come with me."

"I'll come too," Ben stood up.

They joined the firefighters and ambulance paramedics who were already at the scene. They could hear survivors calling out from beneath the rubble and rescued three adults and one child by digging them out with their bare hands, but they could not save anyone from Mrs. Taylor's family. No one slept that night.

The doodlebugs kept coming right over the next few months. It was a long and bitter winter. For weeks at a time, there was snow on the ground. The roads were icy. Fuel shortages meant that buildings were cold and damp. The Bees and Miriam kept their coats on in school because it was so cold. Through it all, the sirens continued sounding and the bombs continued coming.

The damage across London was extensive. Thousands of buildings, commercial and residential, had been razed by the bombs. Those that had escaped destruction often had roof damage or no windows. The butcher commented to Lydia as he wrapped a bone for Winnie, "You know, luv, they say there's not a bus left what's got a pane of glass."

By the time the final two doodlebugs exploded toward the end of March 1945, it seemed like the citizens' morale was as shattered as the buildings. If someone had told Lydia that she would thank God for the end of the war in Britain a scant six weeks later, she would not have believed them.

May 8, 1945, turned out to be one of the happiest days of Lydia's thirty years since Talat Pasha had upended her life. Churchill declared the day a national holiday. Hundreds of thousands of elated citizens took to the streets to celebrate. The six years of war which had cost the lives of millions, and destroyed so many families, homes, and cities, was at an end. People were dancing in the streets and revelling in the pubs. There were parades, street parties, and, importantly for Lydia, thanksgiving services in local churches. The Bees joined in the festivities, but more than ever thought they should now be able to go home.

Two weeks later, a letter arrived from the Bees' Aunt Rachel. It was addressed to Lydia and Dikran. Lydia opened it. Rachel Kleiman first expressed her gratitude to the Vartounians for taking the children, then she wrote that she was planning to travel to London to take Bayla and Ben back to Berlin. They had been sorely missed. She went on to inform the Vartounians, with great regret and sadness, that Bayla and Ben's parents had been deported to Auschwitz. They had not been heard from again and were presumed dead. She herself, she explained, had survived in part because she was in a mixed marriage with an Aryan name. She also had removed the yellow star she had been told to wear, had dyed her hair blond, and had obtained forged documents regarding her birth and maiden name.

Lydia burst into tears. How could she ever tell the Bees? She fervently wished she had waited until Dikran was home to open the letter. How could she explain her tears to the children?

"Dear God, help me." She fell to her knees, sobbing and praying.

Part Four

London to Brighton

1946 - 1958

37

It had been almost a year since the end of the war, but rationing of groceries and widespread destruction remained. Each morning, as Lydia went shopping for that day's milk, bread, and meat, she could not escape seeing the unrepaired houses, the vacant lots, and the war debris strewn across streets and gardens.

Where an apartment building had stood at the end of the block, there was nothing but rubble. Where two homes had been at the other end of her street, there was only debris. Across from the Vartounian's home, three houses were now one pile of rubble. Stray dogs were often wandering through the devastation in search of food. To reach the shops, Lydia could pick her way carefully through vacant lots full of wreckage, or she could take a much longer route. She could do nothing about the continuing shortages of meat, sugar, cheese, and butter.

"Destruction and desolation" she muttered to Winnie as they left the house, "like so much of my life."

"Woof," Winnie responded sympathetically.

Each day when she returned, the house seemed empty to Lydia. Her chores were lessened, with Ben and Bayla having returned to Berlin, but she missed them terribly. Most of all, she missed her son. Leon, her pride and joy, now seventeen-years-old, was away at medical school. Fifteen-year-old Miriam, the only child left in the household, was most often a source of turmoil and anxiety for Lydia.

"I don't know what to do with that child," she complained to Dikran one evening, as they settled into bed. "She's so different from Leon. He was always such a good boy. But Miriam, she doesn't appreciate anything. She never listens. She and that Irish friend of hers, Johnna. Both of them, such smart girls. But always making trouble."

"I know it's been hard on you, Lydia. Miriam can be difficult. But I think she's just a fun-loving teenager—perhaps just a bit too independent? Why don't you write to your friend Sarah about this—maybe she can help. Sarah has always been good for you, hasn't she? I know little about teenage girls."

"I have written to Sarah. But she has no idea. Miriam has all the opportunities for a good life. She is so fortunate. She was lucky to pass the eleven plus exams and go to such an excellent grammar school, but all she does is complain about the uniform, the rules, the teachers. These are not problems. She has nothing to complain about! When I think about my life at her age. I had plenty to complain about, but I didn't. Perhaps I just had no one to complain to." Lydia sighed. "God grant me the patience to deal with her. Maybe I should talk to the priest, but it is embarrassing."

"I'll talk to her about school tomorrow, and maybe we can see what to do. In the meantime, let's try to get some sleep."

The next evening, as he said he would, Dikran raised the subject of school at dinner. He started by asking Miriam what she liked about school.

"I like my friend Johnna." Miriam replied. "She's really nice, she's funny, and she's smart. We have a lot of fun together."

"And what else do you like?" Dikran asked, cutting his stuffed cabbage into bite-sized pieces.

"Nothing."

Asked to elaborate, Miriam indulged in a litany of complaints. Aside from the predictable complaints about the strict discipline and ugly uniform, she commented on what she perceived to be the inanity of the lessons.

"Honestly dad, in domestic science, we have to learn how to iron a man's shirt, sew aprons, darn socks, cook stuff we never eat, and even dumb things like how to lay a table for a dinner party. Why do I need to go to school for that? Mum could teach me that stuff if I wanted to learn it, but I don't. It's like they are trying to turn us into some man's good little wife. Me and Johnna don't want to spend our lives looking after some man and his work mates. We want to travel and see the world and have adventures. Not darn stupid socks and sew stupid aprons." Miriam was getting increasingly agitated.

Dikran tried to hide a smile.

"But one day you will meet and marry a nice Armenian boy, and you'll be glad you know these things." Lydia commented. Miriam snorted.

"Surely some of your lessons are interesting or useful?" Dikran asked, ignoring Lydia. "What about science or history or literature?"

Miriam sighed loudly. "Some of that stuff is okay, but they tell us that we have to learn it so that we can have an intelligent conversation with our husbands." Miriam adopted the voice of one of her teachers "Now now girrrls, you must be good companions when you paaass into the aaafterlife." She mocked.

"Afterlife?" Dikran was puzzled.

"Yea, that's what she calls leaving school. It's stupid! All stupid. And speaking of stupid, Miss Booth said she was gonna teach us about where babies come from. She started by saying she would show us a film. So, there was this woman sitting up in bed and a man in a dressing gown brought her some sorta breakfast on a tray and kissed her. That was it. There were no babies. Just breakfast and a kiss. Does kissing make babies? One of the girls said it does if the girl keeps her mouth open. Miss Booth didn't seem to know. She didn't answer. Anyway, after that, she said something about men having seeds they have to plant. She never said where or how. So, Johnna put up her hand and asked what it means in the Bible when it says something about this man who let his seed fall upon the ground. Are those the seeds you need to grow a baby? Is that how it's done? Did you plant seeds for me, dad?" she asked.

Lydia turned scarlet and gasped. "That's dirty talk," she said. "Stop it at once."

"Yea, well, I guess Miss Booth thought so too. She told Johnna to sit down and be quiet. Then she talked about rabbits—something about oviducts and uteri—whatever they are. Honestly, dad, rabbits! Then she told us it was the same with men and women and she left the room. None of us knew what she was talking about. We just got the giggles. And anyway, mum, what does it mean about spilling seeds—you're always reading the Bible, you must know."

"Stop it, Miriam. You just need to know to stay away from boys. They'll only hurt you. When you're older, we'll find a nice Armenian boy at our church, and you will marry him. Until then, stay away from boys and if one is near you, make sure to keep your legs together. You don't want to get into trouble!"

Miriam, looking askance, pushed her dinner plate away from her, stood up, and left the table. She went into her room, slamming the door as hard as she could.

"You see what I mean, Dikran?" Lydia sighed.

38

"I've been thinking," Dikran said to Lydia, "that you should take a break." As so often happened, it was a day that ended with an intense argument with Miriam, who was now almost seventeen. This time she'd been caught smoking.

"What do you mean?" Lydia was puzzled.

"All through our marriage and all through the war, you've worked hard to look after us all, and Winnie. Everyday you shop and clean and cook. You have never had a day off! Miriam, Winnie, and I can look after ourselves for a week or so. And I thought that you might like to go to Marseille and have a visit with Sarah. What do you think? Would you like that?"

"That's out of the question, Dikran. Miriam would get into all kinds of trouble if I'm not here."

But even as she voiced objections, Lydia could feel a growing surge of excitement at the thought of seeing her oldest and dearest friend. Her confidante. At the end of an hour's discussion of all the things that could go wrong, and what Dikran would do to prevent any catastrophes, it was decided. Lydia's letter to Sarah asking if a visit would be all right was answered by return mail with an enthusiastic yes.

Lydia's excitement at the trip was paralleled by her anxiety over leaving Dikran and Miriam. She made sure her friends from church, and Eva, knew she would be away and had each of them agree to keep an eye out for Miriam and Dikran. She left recipes and shopping lists for Dikran and Miriam to prepare dinners. She scrubbed the house from top to bottom, ensured all the laundry was washed and dried, and weeded her garden thoroughly before leaving. Although only going for a week, she prepared as though it were a month.

On the ship, Lydia thought back to her first trip to Marseille. This trip would be easier because she would not need to use both a train and a ship. She'd booked a direct ship from London to Marseille. She reflected on the dreadful lack of sanitation and the pervasive seasickness of so many women and children on her first ocean voyage. But she also remembered the joy of helping Yasmine give birth and of her pride when Yasmine said she would name her baby after Lydia. She wondered what had happened to Yasmine and her new family. She prayed they had all survived the war and that baby Lydia had grown into a healthy and happy girl. And more obedient than Miriam, she thought. She also reflected on her first trip from Marseille to London—her first sighting of Dikran. It all seemed so long ago. What if she hadn't gone to England, but stayed in Marseille with Sarah? What if she'd stayed in Aleppo? The sound of the ship's horn jolted her out of her musing. They had arrived.

Despite the many years that they had been apart, Lydia and Sarah had no difficulty recognizing each other at the Port of Marseille when Lydia disembarked. The reunion was joyous. Lydia relaxed despite her anxieties about leaving the family. She soon stopped worrying about them.

During the days, Sarah delighted in showing Lydia the Armenian Quarter and the Armenian cathedral and in introducing her to many of the Armenian merchants. Much of the area was being rebuilt after the devastation of the war. It seemed to Lydia that there had been less damage in Marseille than in London. She sensed an energy and a vibrancy that she had not felt in London. Lydia and Sarah went for long walks around the Vieux Port, the old port of Marseille, a natural harbour, and the maritime hub. It was as busy and noisy as London, but Lydia found it more interesting and captivating; it was also warmer and the air felt cleaner.

Lydia enjoyed the cafes and the fresh bouillabaisse that was served with crusty French bread and a dollop of rouille on top. Lydia had never tasted anything like it and was keen to know how to make it. Sarah explained they would make it with whatever fish they could find, although tuna was her favourite, with a couple of potatoes and onions.

"Of course," she added, "lots of garlic and fresh herbs. This is France, none of your bland English food."

During the evenings, they reminisced and listened to music. Sarah had recently purchased a record player. Lydia was fascinated with it and loved that they could just be at home listening to the most wonderful sounds. Sarah had only a few records, but there were two that she played repeatedly.

Lydia's favourite was Beniamino Gigli singing the aria "E lucevan le stelle" from Puccini's opera *Tosca*. Each time she listened to it, she felt deep emotion and became teary. She had never heard anything more beautiful. Sarah's favourite was Johann Strauss' "Emperor Waltz". Lydia enjoyed it immensely, but it did not move her the way the Puccini aria did. She decided to ask Dikran if they could buy a record player just as soon as she returned. Maybe if she could listen to Puccini, she could cope better with Miriam. Maybe the music of Puccini would be the antidote she needed to the nightmares. She would also get a recording of the Ode to Joy; she still hummed it to herself when anxious or upset.

Their most meaningful times, however, were not those spent in exploring neighbourhoods or listening to music, or even attending services at the cathedral, but in conversation. They talked at length about their shared childhood experiences in Zeitun. They shared their memories of Mrs. Sarkissian in Aleppo. And they shared their subsequent vastly different experiences.

Their adult lives had taken very different trajectories. Each had ended up with what the other had wanted. Sarah had been the one who wanted marriage and children. But after her husband had died, she remained alone and was happy being a teacher. Lydia had wanted to stay alone and be a teacher. But she had married and had children. Clearly, she thought, God's plans for us were not the same as ours.

Lydia knew little of Sarah's daily life other than she was enjoying the Armenian community and her teaching position. On the other hand, Sarah was familiar with Lydia's daily life, as much had been shared in letters. But Lydia had written little about her memories and her fears. These she shared in person. For the first time, she talked to Sarah at length about her parents, her brother, her Aunt Ruth, and baby Ani.

"You know, Sarah, what I wish most is that I could find my brother, Luke. What happened to him and my parents? I hate not knowing. There is such a gap in my life—I can't fill it. I love my kids and my husband, and even my dog, but oh how I long for my family—at least to know what happened. I have prayed so often for some knowledge. What if Luke is still alive and I could see him, but I don't know where he is?"

"I understand Lydia. I love being here—there are so many Armenians, it sort of feels like home, but I too have so many gaps in my memories." She paused. "Do you suppose we could go to Zeitun? Just for a visit, of course, although I hear there are many Armenians who are repatriating. I wonder if we could trace what happened to our families. But...." Sarah paused and sighed heavily.

"Yes, I know what you're thinking, Sarah. Armenia is under Soviet control now. We'd probably not be safe."

"Maybe not. We would have to be very careful about what we said and what questions we asked. Did you hear about that writer and history professor Zabel Yesayan? Like us, she escaped the genocide. But then she went back from here to Armenia. Although some people argued it wasn't true, I heard that almost as soon as she got there, the Russians exiled her to Siberia. I didn't hear anything more. I don't know if anyone did. It seems like anyone they see as a patriotic Armenian may be in danger of being sent to Siberia. And who knows what happens then?"

"I can't risk it. I have to stay safe, Sarah. I have my daughter to care for still. And Dikran"

Agreeing it would be too risky, they dismissed the idea of travel to Zeitun but decided that at some point Sarah would travel to England to meet Lydia's family.

The night before Lydia was due to travel home, Sarah talked about her experience through the Second World War. Lydia was astonished and impressed to learn that Sarah had played an active role in the French Resistance. Lydia had always believed that other than her teaching, Sarah lived a quiet life. Reality was far different.

Sarah told Lydia that she had been recruited by the Armenian writer and poet, Louise Aslanian, who had opened the woman's division of the Resistance. It had been dangerous, frightening, exciting and satisfying, Sarah explained. She had been fortunate to stay safe. Sadly, she explained to Lydia, both Louise and her husband Arpia had not been so lucky. In July of 1944, they had been arrested, and then in early 1945, they were killed in Nazi concentration camps.

"Oh Sarah, must our stories always end with violence and death?" Lydia sat with tears running down her face.

Lydia sailed from Marseille back to London feeling refreshed but also uneasy, despite the Puccini. The conversations with Sarah had evoked a lot of memories that she had been repressing. They were difficult to deal with. The nightmares had returned a few days before her return. Once again, she was reliving the rapes, the intense fear, hunger, and anxiety crossing the desert, and the deep sadness of losing her family. She was relieved that she and Sarah had decided against a trip to Armenia. Lydia did not feel strong enough to deal with the emotions she knew such a trip would evoke. She worried that the nightmares and flashbacks would continue after she was home from a trip to her homeland. It would be hard on Dikran.

Waiting for a taxi, she turned her thoughts to her family. She wondered what the state of the house would be after her absence. How messy would it be? Would Winnie have been fed? Would Miriam have caused problems for Dikran? Her anxiety increased as the cab driver maneuvered the car through the busy streets.

39

Lydia's concerns vanished as soon as she arrived home. The first to welcome her as the taxi dropped her off at their house was Winnie, wagging his tail and happily whimpering. Dikran and Miriam were not far behind. Lydia was pleased and somewhat surprised to see that all was well. The house was clean and tidy. In the week that Lydia had been gone, Miriam had learned to cook a few meals. She had a lamb stew simmering on the stove when Lydia walked in. It smelled wonderful.

She was happy to be back with her family. Being away had made her realize how much she had come to find pleasure in being with Dikran. That night, after enjoying making love with him, Lydia slept well. She awoke refreshed and content.

The next day, Miriam surprised Lydia again.

"I'm getting a job, mum." Miriam sounded pleased with herself. "I'm going to become a stewardess, and so is Johnna, and then we can fly around the world and have lots of adventures."

"What?" Lydia was stunned. "You have no qualifications for such a dangerous job."

"Yes, I do, mum. They said I was the right height and weight and would look really good in the uniform. And they're going to train me in how to deal with first aid and things like men who pinch your bottom." She laughed. "I can't wait."

Lydia was speechless. She could not fathom being more surprised. But yet another surprise awaited her.

"There's a letter here you might want to read." Dikran said with a smile. He handed her an envelope. The postmark indicated it was from

Leon. She tore into it and quickly started reading. Lydia was thrilled to read that Leon was coming home for a visit. They had rarely seen him over the past two years while he had been studying at medical school. Although it was in London, Leon stayed in a boarding house beside the campus. He had told Lydia that he had insufficient free time to come home except between semesters, and then only if he did not have to spend time at a hospital. As she read on, Lydia became even more excited. Leon wrote that he wanted to bring with him his girlfriend to meet the family.

"Oh Dikran" Lydia said, "did you read this? Can you believe it? Our dear son has an Armenian girlfriend! I'm so happy."

Miriam groaned and announced she was taking Winnie for a walk before dinner.

Her name, Leon had written, was Dalita Krikorian. Her parents were from Yerevan. They had lived in Brighton for the past three years. Leon had met Dalita, an only child, at the medical school. She had chosen the Royal Free Hospital School of Medicine because it was the first teaching hospital in London to admit women. But by the time she started in 1948, all the medical schools were co-ed.

She had just started her training when Leon met her. He had seen her studying in the library. His first thought was that she looked Armenian. The second was that she was beautiful and, given that she was studying at medical school, she must be intelligent. He took a chance, walked up to her, and introduced himself. It was, they agreed later, love at first sight. She's so lovely, Leon had written, very smart and very kind. She wants to work with children after she gets her medical degree. He expressed his belief that the family would love her as much as he did. He couldn't wait to introduce her to them all.

Lydia decided that inviting her for a good Armenian dinner would be the best way to meet her. The date was set. Lydia took what she had left of her linens and lace work out of storage, where she had been keeping them. She carefully washed and ironed them so that they would be fresh and ready to adorn the dinner table. She found two tall silver candlesticks at a second-hand store. After she had thoroughly polished them, they would be placed in the middle of the table, with small jars of fresh flowers on either side. Dikran asked if she would like to have a bottle of wine for the occasion. Lydia was torn. She had always expressed a belief that drinking alcohol was for sinners. She decided that God would be okay with them having a small glass of wine to celebrate the occasion. Days were then spent preparing a traditional Armenian meal as best she could, given the continuing food rations.

Lydia was anxious when the day finally came. She imagined everything that could possibly go wrong. None if it did. Dalita was as delightful as Leon had described. There was a lot of cheerful conversation and laughter over dinner. Even Miriam, Lydia noted, seemed to be charmed by Dalita. Lydia could not have been happier. That night, she prayed that the two would get married and make her a grandmother.

"If only Miriam would find a nice Armenian boy and settle down instead of this silly stewardess nonsense."

"She's still young, Lydia." Dikran reminded her.

"Old enough to get into trouble."

Six months later, Leon and Dalita were engaged. They arranged to hold their wedding at the church Lydia continued to attend regularly—St. Sarkis Armenian Church in London. The Krikorians were delighted with the arrangement. They had already visited with the Vartounians. The two families liked each other immediately and both were happy with the match. Lydia thought how perfect it would have been if only the Krikorians had a son of the right age for Miriam.

The boy Miriam was dating was English rather than Armenian. Lydia had only met him once and then briefly, but she had determined that he was totally unacceptable for her daughter. He had come to the door one evening to pick Miriam up and take her out. Lydia did not approve.

"He looks weird, don't you think, Dikran?" Lydia asked after she met him. "He was dressed in the strangest clothes."

"Many young men do these days, Miriam," Dikran replied. "I think they are just tired of drab uniforms, rationing, and the sort of suits their dads' wear. I noticed the menswear shops of East and South London are selling Edwardian style suits at very cheap prices. Anyway, what's important is that he seems like an okay boy. He's a butcher, so he'll have no difficulty having a job. There're still shortages after the war took so many lives. I think many of the young ones today are just having fun with clothes."

"So, you don't think he's a hooligan?" Lydia was concerned.

"I don't think so, and Miriam is happier than she has been for a long time. Just leave it, Lydia. She's finished her training and soon she'll be busy flying. She'll soon forget about this Johnny—isn't that his name?"

* * *

"Johnny's got a job in Canada," Miriam announced at dinner a few weeks after Leon and Dalita's wedding, a joyous occasion at St. Sarkis Church.

"That's good," said Lydia, feeling very relieved.

"And I'm going with him." Miriam stated emphatically. "We think it's time to get out of England. How can you stand it? All the bombed-out houses, all the shortages, the rationing. Johnny can't even get a decent job here, and we can't find anywhere to live. We want to get married and have a decent life. There's lots of jobs in Canada, and there's loads of houses. We saw the men at the immigration office in Piccadilly. They said so."

Six weeks later, Lydia and Dikran were standing at the Port of Southampton waving goodbye to Miriam and Johnny, who had embarked on a ship bound for Montreal. Nothing they had said or threatened had weakened Miriam's resolve to leave with Johnny. Lydia could only pray that her daughter was not making a huge mistake. She had tried so hard to keep her family together. Despite the anxieties Miriam had caused her, Lydia didn't want Miriam to leave. She had never wanted either of her children to be far away. Now it seemed like they would both be gone. Must she always lose everyone she loved?

40

Lydia now only had to shop and cook for her and Dikran. Rationing continued, but only needing food for two made shopping easier. Winnie continued to accompany her on her daily trips to the shops. She was glad to have him and enjoyed his company. But, with only an occasional short visit from Leon and a rare letter from the Bees, she felt lonely. With neither the war, nor a house full of children, Lydia returned to playing the piano, and to attending church services more regularly. Neither activity compensated for the absence of her children, but they helped keep her calm.

She got a great deal of pleasure out of listening to records on the player that Dikran had bought for her after she had told him how much she loved listening to the music at Sarah's. With the player, Dikran had purchased for her a copy of Beethoven's "Ode to Joy." She had told him one day about how much she had loved it as a child and how she was preparing for her violin solo when the soldiers came.

The first time she played the record, she was transported to the day she and Anoush met the goatherder—the day when she had cradled newborn Ani to her chest to hide her. She recalled how she would hum it the nights she was Hayriye being abused. They were difficult memories. She wondered what had happened to Ani and prayed that she had been well cared for. In the afternoons, she would play her recordings of Puccini arias and of Handel's *Messiah*. She would sing along with the aria, "I know that my Redeemer Liveth." The music filled her soul.

The first letter from Miriam did not arrive for a full three months after she had left Southampton. Lydia was delighted to hear from her at last. In the letter, Miriam described their journey. Johnny's new boss had agreed to pay for their passage if she agreed to work in his shop for six months with no additional pay. Miriam had agreed, even though he had only paid for them to travel in steerage. She wrote that she was surprised how much fun they had in steerage. There had been lots of other young couples around, and they had enjoyed their time despite the discomforts and the rough seas across the Atlantic. Her big news was that they had asked the ship's captain to marry them.

"Listen Dikran," Lydia said, as she read from the letter. "We got married in the ship's ballroom with the Captain and the Chaplain doing the ceremony. Lots of our new friends hung around, and they all clapped and cheered. One of them had a harmonica. He played it after, and we all danced. It was so much fun." Lydia stopped reading and turned to Dikran.

"Is she married in the eyes of God Dikran, or is she living in sin?"

Dikran assured her that given that they had been married by a chaplain, God would be okay with the marriage ceremony not being in a church.

After being processed at immigration at the Port of Montreal, Miriam had continued, they took the train all the way across Canada to Vancouver. It took almost a week, she wrote, the country is so big.

"Dikran," Lydia sounded surprised, "she says that the houses they saw from the train were made of wood. What sort of house is that—a shed? Wouldn't they catch fire? And for one day they saw only poles in fields. What a strange place that Canada must be. But oh, listen to this." She read.

When we got to the west, there were mountains, really big ones with snow on the top. I remembered once, mum, you talked about a mountain. I think it was called Arat or something. I wondered if your mountain was like these ones we saw? Johnny and me couldn't believe how big they are.

The letter finished with little information about where they were living, but with a promise of a second letter soon. Lydia knew they lived in Vancouver from the return address but knew nothing about it. Was it a big city? Were there mountains or rivers, what were the people who lived there like? She wanted answers. At least she knew they had arrived safely in their strange new land. Lydia was comforted by that. But she remained disturbed about the lack of a proper church wedding and prayed that Dikran was right, and that God would forgive Miriam for her rebellious and non-Christian behaviour.

* * *

Four months passed before a second letter arrived. In it, Miriam described how different she found everything in Vancouver compared to London. They were doing okay with their jobs, she wrote, but some differences took getting used to.

"So, this one day, I told my boss that Johnny had knocked me up that morning." Lydia was reading the letter to Dikran. "The boss looked shocked and asked how I could know. I told him cos I got up in time to get to work without being late. He finally figured out what I meant and told me that in Canada "knocking someone up" means getting them pregnant, not waking them up in the morning so they're not late for work. I was so embarrassed."

Lydia was mortified. Dikran chuckled.

Miriam had gone on to explain other words that were different. She listed some. Lydia read on.

> Your car boot is a trunk, the pavement is the sidewalk, a lorry is a truck, and a chemist is a drugstore. It's so weird. And the cars here are so big you could land a helicopter on the boot—oops, trunk. And a lot of people here say they can't understand me and Johnny cos of our accents! Crazy!

"Does she write about the things she likes?" Dikran asked Lydia, who was clutching the letter and seemed determined to read it before Dikran.

"She says there's lots of space everywhere, and oh Dikran, she is so lucky. She has a refrigerator in her flat, though she calls it her apartment, so she doesn't have to go shopping for food every day. And, she says, there's lots of food and no line-ups. Think of that Dikran. Just being able to go to the butcher's and buy what you want. Here Dikran," Lydia handed the letter to him after she finished it, "you can read it. Leon and Dalita will be here soon so they can read it too when they come."

Lydia left Dikran reading the letter and went to prepare dinner for the four of them. She was very much looking forward to seeing her son and his wife. They would be amused by Miri's letter, she thought. They were, but they had news of their own.

Leon had been offered and had accepted a position at a children's hospital in Brighton. It was exactly the type of position he had hoped and trained for, and he was ecstatic. Dalita had been interviewed for a position in a nearby medical clinic and they were waiting to hear about that. They were hopeful. Their move, they explained, would be easy since Dalita's parents had lots of space in their house and were happy to have them stay there until they found their own flat or house. Lydia was happy for them but saddened that they would be leaving London. She wondered how often she would be able to see them.

"My family is being torn apart again," she muttered to no one in particular. "Always apart."

"Don't look so sad, mum, it's only an hour on the train. You and dad can come and visit whenever you want."

"I have news too." Dalita spoke up. "You two are going to be grand-parents next spring."

41

In January of 1952, the Vartounian family received a long letter from Bayla and Ben. They were still living in Berlin, and they were doing well, they wrote. The big news was that Ben was getting married. He really hoped that the Vartounians could attend the wedding and act as the surrogate parents he perceived them to be. Bayla invited them to stay at her flat in central Berlin. Dikran and Lydia agreed that it would be wonderful to see the Bees again, and a privilege to attend Ben's wedding in place of his late parents.

"Dikran, maybe we could go by boat to France and then train to Berlin. It would be like us having a holiday together—we never have."

"I'll have to check with work, Lydia."

While Dikran looked into the possibility of him taking some time off work, Lydia searched for information about Berlin in the newspapers at the local library.

"Good news, Lydia," Dikran said when he got home that evening. "I can get a couple of weeks off with no problem."

"That's good to know," Lydia said, not looking pleased as Dikran had expected. "Dikran," she said, "I spent hours today reading about Berlin and I don't like what I learned. Even though the war is over, there are continuing tensions between the East Berlin and West Berlin. I got a feeling that it's dangerous there. I didn't read all the political details, but it looks like since the allies took control of the west and the Soviet Union the east, there've been lots of problems, and—."

"No way are we going if there is any danger," Dikran interrupted her. "It would be lovely to see the Bees, but I will not do anything that puts you in harm's way. You have experienced too much hurt, my dear Lydia. I love you and as I promised so long ago, I will protect you always to the best of my ability. Please write to the Bees and explain that we cannot come, and of course, wish them well. Maybe we can go visit them in a year or two when things settle."

Lydia was disappointed but also relieved that she would be sure to be in England when Dalita's baby was born, whether it was early or late.

* * *

Dalita's pregnancy progressed well. Her final trimester at the beginning of nineteen fifty-two had been a time of preparation. Leon had found them a house near the hospital where he was working. They had moved in right after Christmas and taken great delight in preparing a room for the baby. Dalita's parents, Narek and Milena Krikorian had invited Lydia and Dikran to stay with them in Brighton. This invitation was happily accepted. They decided to go a few days before the due date and then stay the full two weeks of vacation time that Dikran had been allowed. They would have a vacation, after all.

The two families got to know each other as they helped prepare for the birth. The two grandmothers spent many hours sharing information about their childhoods in Armenia. They laughed at their shared childhood fantasies of climbing Ararat, and Lydia told Milena about her brother thinking Noah should have had dinosaurs on the ark. What they avoided talking about was their experiences through the years of the genocide. There seemed to be an unspoken agreement that they would limit their conversations to pleasant topics. Neither wanted memories to spoil the happiness each was feeling with their new sense of broadened and cohesive family.

While Milena and Lydia were preparing the house and baby's room, Narek and Dikran worked in the garden. Like Dikran, Narek had taken time from his job. He was an accounting clerk. They worked together to fix the fencing around the back garden and to build a swing for the baby. They also dug an area and planted runner beans, tomatoes, and carrots. While they worked, they talked about their experiences with immigration and shared their hopes for the futures of their children and future grandchildren. Each day when they finished, they took some time to visit the local pubs and enjoyed relaxing over a beer.

* * *

Dalita woke at three in the morning on March twentieth, feeling what she initially thought were stomach cramps. She soon realized she was in labour. By noon, her contractions were close enough together that it was time for Leon to take her to the hospital. Dalita was glad her parents had a telephone. She called them and all four parents went at once to the maternity hospital. They met Leon in the waiting room, and all spent the next four hours anxiously waiting news of Dalita and the baby.

When the doctor finally came into the room, the smile on his face was the broadest any of them had ever seen.

"Congratulations, young man." He said, shaking Leon's hand. "You have a son," he paused and grinned as they all cheered, "and," he continued, "a daughter."

Leon paled. "What did you say?"

"Yes son. Your wife has just given birth to the two healthiest twin babies I have ever delivered. One boy and one girl. Are you ready to meet them?"

The Krikorians and the Vartounians looked at each other. They were as elated as they were surprised. They were all speechless. Leon went with the doctor. He returned about twenty minutes later. None had ever seen him look so happy.

"You can come and meet your granddaughter, Gemma, and your grandson, Emin, now." He led them into the nursery.

They all agreed it was the best surprise of their lives. Although small, the babies appeared to be robust. They each had a shock of jet-black hair, although Gemma had more than Emin.

"Perhaps that's how we'll be able to tell them apart," said Lydia, staring adoringly at the babies.

Dalita stayed in the hospital for ten days. Leon was at work, so the grandparents divided up the shopping that had been necessitated by the unexpected arrival of two babies. By the time Dalita brought Gemma and Emin home, there were two cribs ready, a mobile hung over each of them, and a teddy bear sat in each. Two sets of clothing had been purchased, as well as several boxes of disposal nappies and some cloth ones. Lydia had not heard of disposable nappies before and thought how much easier they made a mother's day. She recalled the ever-present bucket of water with bleach full of smelly nappies waiting for her to scrub them clean.

They exchanged the pram that had been purchased for one that would accommodate two infants. The house had been cleaned and the furniture polished. Lydia had also made some dinners that could easily be heated, which she placed in their refrigerator. Lydia was as impressed with the refrigerator as she had been with the disposable nappies. The Krikorians, she a schoolteacher and he a clerk, had done well.

* * *

Once Dalita came home, Lydia and Dikran had only a few days left in Brighton. Lydia spent them with Milena, helping Dalita with the babies and the daily household chores. They reflected on how well everyone had got along and how pleased they were that Leon and Dalita had appreciated their involvement, not seen it as interference. They vowed to see each other again as soon as possible. In the meantime, Milena promised to write weekly letters to Lydia to keep her updated on the twins' progress.

"That might have been the happiest two weeks of my life," Lydia told Dikran, on the train back to London. "Even though I'm exhausted, it was so hard to leave. I wish we were nearer so we see them often. With my asthma, travel is too tiring. I don't think I could manage day trips. Isn't it wonderful that our dear Leon married such a lovely Armenian girl? And what a nice family she comes from. If only Miriam...." She sighed.

As soon as they got home, Lydia wrote a long letter to Sarah telling her all about the babies. She wrote also to Miriam. In her letter, she stressed that Miriam was always welcome to come home and how nice it would be for the twins to have their aunt around.

42

Back in London, Lydia was upset to find that Winnie, who had been staying with neighbours during their absence, was not well. He seemed reluctant to move. He yelped when Lydia touched him, and he was limping. She took him to the vet, who diagnosed Winnie with advanced arthritis. Since he was obviously in a lot of pain and relatively old, the vet recommended euthanizing him. The house became even quieter.

Her own health issues intensified the loneliness and depression Lydia had been feeling since their return from Brighton. Her asthma had been getting worse. It seemed worse in London than it had in Brighton. Lydia wondered if it was the way she was feeling or the difference in climate. The seaside air had felt fresher than that of the big city. Her doctor had prescribed aminophylline suppositories and tablets, as well as epinephrine injections. She used them all. They provided little relief. She struggled to go to the shops each day and to continue growing vegetables and flowers in the garden.

Her highlight each week was the letter that Milena Krikorian wrote, as she had promised, with details of the twins. Lydia was especially thrilled one morning when she opened the letter and photos of Gemma and Emin smiling fell out onto the table. The twins were now three months old. The photo suggested they were catching up to normal size and were very healthy. In her letter, Milena told Lydia that the following month, Dalita would work two days a week, not at the clinic where she had interviewed previously, but at the same hospital as Leon. Milena would look after the twins.

Lydia was pleased that Milena could take care of her grandchildren and was confident in her capacity to do so. She also felt a twinge of envy. How she would have loved to be a more active part of their lives.

Lydia wondered if Miriam would have children with Johnny and if she did, would she raise them in Canada? She had not heard much from Miriam for a long time. Rather than send full letters, Miriam sent the occasional postcard with various pictures of the Vancouver area where she was still living. The messages were terse. All Lydia knew about Miriam was where she lived. The area looked beautiful, and Lydia wished she could go there and see it and see how her daughter was doing. The lack of personal detail from Miriam worried Lydia. She suspected that the marriage was not working out. But even if they had the money for the fare, and Dikran could get enough time off work, she did not feel strong enough to undertake such a journey.

Although she often had found Miriam a challenge and a source of frustration, she hoped Miriam would return one day. She never stopped wanting every member of her family close by. Each night, she prayed that Miriam would be safe and well and come home. She again wrote to Miriam, stressing how nice it would be to have her back home with them.

The winter of nineteen fifty-two was unusually cold and damp, even for London. Each day was more of a struggle for Lydia to do the shopping. She was only forty-eight years old, but she felt like an old woman. Dikran, five years older than Lydia, seemed much younger. But even he had trouble breathing on the days when there was heavy fog.

December that year was the most health-challenging they had faced. Dikran arrived home late and upset on Friday, December fifth. His trousers were torn, and his knees were bleeding. Lydia was shocked.

"I couldn't see where I was walking," he explained. "The fog is so thick. I don't think I've ever seen it this bad before. I fell off the curb into the road. It really hurt. My knees are a right mess! It's a good thing there were no cars coming or I'd be in real trouble."

"Let me clean you up, Dikran. Looks like there's some gravel in your cuts. We'd better clean that out. I have some Dettol to disinfect them." Dikran sat on a chair in the kitchen while Lydia washed the gravel from his knees and applied disinfectant to them. He winced as it stung. She decided she would sew knee patches on his trousers later.

"You know, Dikran," she said, ignoring his wincing, "I too had difficulty this morning. I could still see okay, though in places it was difficult, but the fog was so thick my asthma was terrible."

The density of, and the danger posed by, the fog were increasingly obvious over the weekend. The fog did not dissipate. It got worse. By Sunday, it had even penetrated their home. They could smell it and taste it, and Lydia was increasingly having trouble breathing. Dikran and Lydia listened to the news on the radio to get information about what to expect. If the fog was going to get any worse, Lydia might have to go to the hospital.

What they heard was disturbing. The BBC announcer started by warning the public to stay indoors. It was, he said, the worst smog ever experienced in the country. It had not only been very cold, he explained, but there had been no wind. As a result, all the coal fires people were burning to keep warm meant there was more smoke than ever in the air. This was, he continued, mixing with other particles in the air, like motor vehicle exhausts and smoke from industrial chimneys. With no wind to disburse the smoke, and with the fog, there was an unprecedented number of pollutants in the air. "It is expected to last until the middle of next week," he concluded.

"What shall we do, Dikran? I cannot breathe in this." Lydia was tearful.

Dikran suggested she sit in the bathroom for a while. There were no windows, so it might have less smog than the other rooms in the house.

"If you aren't better tomorrow, we'll take you to the hospital. They will help you."

* * *

The next morning, they learned that getting to the hospital—or anywhere—would be almost impossible. Visibility had become so poor that driving was not an option. Transportation was at a standstill. There were no cars on the road. The buses had stopped running. Even the ambulance service was stopped. Walking, as Dikran had found out days earlier, was dangerous. There was no choice but to stay indoors. Using remnants of their old gas masks from the war, Dikran put together a makeshift mask to help Lydia breathe. It provided some relief. Fortunately, they had enough tinned food in the house that they could eat for a few days. It would not be the fresh and nutritious meals Lydia usually prepared, but it would suffice.

Ten days later, there was still coal dust everywhere, inside and out. Every object in the house and everything Lydia touched on her way to the shops and at the shops was filthy. She decided she could no longer live in such a place. That evening, she asked Dikran if he would find a job in Brighton. They would move there. They must move there. She would miss her priest and St. Sarkis Church. She would miss her friend Eva even though, since Eva and Raffi had moved further away the previous year, they no longer met for lunches. But she could be close to her beloved son, daughter-in-law, and grandchildren. And she would be close to who she believed would become her closest confidant and friend next to Sarah, Milena. And perhaps most important, she could breathe.

43

Dikran was less keen on moving, since he had a senior position and enjoyed his colleagues. However, during the next weeks, as the details of the now called killer fog came to light, he decided Lydia was right. The estimates were that about four thousand people had died from the five days of intense fog, and an incredible one hundred thousand had been made ill. Lydia was not alone. It was, the government admitted, the very worst air pollution in the history of the country.

It took a full year for Dikran to find employment in Brighton, to sell their house in London, and to buy one in Brighton. It was a year in which Lydia became both increasingly impatient and increasingly hopeful. They moved at the beginning of nineteen fifty-four. Dikran started his new position as Senior Inspector of transit a week after the move.

The house they purchased was a small two-bedroom with a tiny garden. But it was between the homes of the Krikorians and Leon and his family. Lydia could not have been happier. Except for Miriam, the people she loved most were now all in walking distance and, without the pea-soup fogs she had endured in London, walking was a pleasure. Lydia enjoyed being close to the ocean. The air felt cleaner and fresher than it had in London and her asthma improved. There was a bus stop one block from their home. Dikran told her which bus she should take to go to the promenade—the stop that was closest to the Palace Pier. She grew very fond of walking in that area. She marvelled at how the pier had survived the war. Overall, she noted, there were many fewer bombed-out areas around her new home than there had been in

London. She had not noticed this on her earlier visit to Brighton, but she reminded herself that she had been preoccupied with the babies.

She was not as close to the shops as she had been in London, but she did not need to be. The house they had purchased had come with a refrigerator which was just the right size to hold a jug of milk, some meat, fish, and two bags of vegetables. Meat was still rationed, so she would buy what she could when it was available and store it in the refrigerator. Milk was delivered to her doorstep each morning and then placed in the refrigerator. She loved the taste of the cold milk, and that she never had to worry about it going sour before it was used up.

She missed St. Sarkis Church. The Krikorians were not regular churchgoers, so they were unable to advise her on where to worship. She tried three different churches during the first month of living in Brighton. The one she settled on was an Evangelical Church. It was within walking distance of their home, and the pastor and his flock had been very welcoming to her. Best of all, they had asked her if she knew how to play the piano. They needed someone to accompany the choir on the weekly hymn rehearsals.

Another happy event in Lydia's life after the move came when Dikran surprised her by purchasing a television set. A small box with rabbit ears antenna, it sat in a corner of the living room. They received two channels. They would relax in the evenings watching the news and quiz shows on the government run television channel, the BBC. On weekends, Dikran would spend some afternoons watching soccer or horse racing. Sunday evenings, they watched the variety show *Sunday Night at the London Palladium* on the other channel they received, the independent channel, ITV. Each week, Lydia commented on how disgusting the dancers were kicking their legs so high you could see their underwear. It was a source of constant amusement to Dikran.

The biggest and most thrilling change for Lydia was her proximity to the twins. She was particularly excited about being there for their second birthday. It was on a Saturday, a day they all had free. Dalita had been quite happy to let the grandmothers plan a family party for Gemma and

Emin. They took the children to the park, where they enjoyed a pony ride, swings, and a sandbox. The six adults were just enough to ensure the rambunctious independence-seeking twins were safe.

It seemed to Lydia that with the twins, there was constant chaos. Overall, it was a happy, albeit noisy, chaos. Gemma and Emin lived in the moment. They had developed the ability to run around and to climb onto furniture, but they could not express their wishes by talking. Frustration was common. But their giggles and joy were much more in evidence than tantrums. Lydia thanked God for them daily and hoped that they, unlike their parents and grandparents, would grow up in a peaceful rather than war-torn society. Each time she played with them, she thought of Luke and Miriam. Had Luke ever become a father? Had Miriam and Johnny had any children? She still did not know if Miriam was okay. She still longed for information about Luke.

Lydia and Dikran's gift for the twins' birthday included professionally taken photographs. They had one photo of the twins, one of the twins with their parents, and one of the entire family. Looking at the photo of the children, Lydia remembered the only time she had her photograph taken. She had been so worried about her tattoos, and so afraid of leaving Aleppo for England and the stranger whose name was Dikran. How well everything had worked out, she thought. She had worried needlessly. The tattoos had largely faded, no one had mentioned them in years, and Dikran had turned out to be a wonderful husband and father. God had truly blessed her.

Dikran ordered extra copies of the photo so that each of the three families had a copy and so that there was an extra one for Lydia to send to Miriam. In her letter to Miriam, Lydia told Miriam about the birthday party, her father's new job, and their new house. And yet again, she stressed how much she would like Miriam to return to England and assured her that there was always room for her in their home. She also reminded her of the importance of family, and, not for the first time, asked Miriam if she had any children. She again prayed that Miriam would understand and come home.

That summer, Dalita returned to work four days a week. The hospital had guaranteed her day shifts only. Milena and Lydia spent two days each at the twins' home caring for them. Lydia enjoyed every minute, even when they were crying or fighting. She would calm them with hugs and songs, and the reading of Bible stories. Milena was more likely to take the twins out in the pram. They often objected to getting in it, but usually settled down and seemed to enjoy themselves smiling at passersby. Milena would talk to them as she walked, telling them the names of the things and people they passed. She was thrilled one day when Gemma pointed at a double-decker and said, "bus." She was amused when Emin pointed at a postman and announced loudly, "daddy."

Over time, more often than not, the two grandmothers would both spend the days with the twins. While the infants had their afternoon naps, the women shared their stories and discussed the diaspora while they drank tea. As they had got to know each other better, they had become more comfortable talking about their pasts—issues they had avoided previously. They now talked at length about their lack of family connection and sense of belonging after Talat Pasha had torn apart their families. The women shared the struggles they had undergone to adapt to a new country and new language. They talked about how they longed to go back and find their childhood homes and families, and how impossible that was.

Lydia confessed how she never stopped wondering what happened to her parents and her brother Luke. They marvelled at how fortunate they were now to have blended their families and above all that Gemma and Emin would grow surrounded by loving extended family. She told Milena about Miriam being sad not to have an extended family. It was hard. Milena empathized. Extended family was something neither had experienced beyond early childhood. It was something sorely missed and highly valued.

Lydia divulged a lot, but not the rapes. After that evening, so many years ago, when she talked to Eva about life with the Yavuz family, and the one time she had talked with the priest, she had never again been able to summon the strength to mention the rapes, other than sharing her nightmares and flashbacks in general terms in her in letters to Sarah. Even when visiting with Sarah, Lydia avoided discussion of her abuse. Milena's experiences through the genocide had been less harsh than those of Lydia, but her sense of loss was similar. Milena was only eight years old when she was taken from her parents and Yerevan. But she had been taken in by a kind Turkish family who had never abused her.

"I was luckier than many," Milena acknowledged. "I had to work in their home and on their farm, but they never hurt me."

"Did you look after cows or sheep?" Lydia interrupted, wanting to focus on something more positive. "I grew to love them when I lived on the farm with the Aydin family."

"I spent little time with the livestock, but I recall one cow who had the most beautiful eyes. I understand why you'd fall in love with them. Anyway, I was there until the Mudros Armistice. I met Narek in Turkey. After we married, we moved to Marseille. We thought it would be safer than Turkey. We came to England in nineteen forty-seven when Dalita was eighteen. She wanted to go to medical school and London seemed like the best option for her, so we moved here. We have been restless, but now we have more of a sense of family. We shall stay here."

44

By the time the twins were four, they were going to nursery school each morning. Milena would pick them up from their home and walk them to school. Lydia would pick them up from school and walk them home. The afternoons continued as before. The children napped while their grandmothers talked about Armenia. It was an arrangement that worked well for everyone. Dalita was now working five days a week, continuing with dayshifts only. Leon alternated between day and night shifts.

The twins continued to be a source of great joy. They were lively, curious, and mischievous. Each Friday, Lydia wrote to both Sarah and Miriam, describing the twins' exploits of the week. She also wrote about their progress in talking, physical activities, and music. Lydia had been teaching them some Armenian words and Armenian children's hymns. She thought about teaching Gemma some simple sewing or knitting but realized that Gemma would unlikely be able to keep still long enough for such activities. Thinking back to how much joy Miriam and Leon had got from Winnie, Lydia asked Leon and Dalita if she could get the children a puppy. Dalita wanted to wait until they were at least six. She thought Gemma might be too aggressive while playing and the puppy could get hurt.

Gemma was dominant, often ordering her brother around. Emin frequently ignored her.

"You are being a pain, child." Gemma said crossly one day, imitating her mother. Dikran, who had overheard the remark, commented that the twins had become the family's primary source of entertainment. "They're more fun than the television," he said. Lydia agreed.

Lydia had mixed feelings about watching television. It could be very entertaining and relaxing. She found more and more that she would be physically tired after her days with the children, and emotionally drained from her conversations with Milena. It was nice to just sit after the evening meal and watch the television. But so often, what she saw and heard on the news distressed her. She worried about her friends and church colleagues who were still living in London, where the terrible fogs continued. She thanked God daily that she no longer had to try to breathe in the foul peasoupers that she had endured, but she was concerned about her old friend from the boarding house, Eva.

Lydia had stayed in touch with Eva over the years, although the socializing between the Vartounians and Eva and Raffi Kevorkian had waned during the war and as each couple's children grew. Her letters to Eva were neither regular nor frequent, like those she wrote to Sarah. With Eva, she wrote only when she had something specific to share or ask. She did write to Eva right after watching a news report about a heavy fog affecting the London area in early December of 1957. She had been shocked to hear that two trains had collided in the dense fog; that almost one hundred people had been killed and another almost two hundred injured. She knew that Raffi used the trains a lot. She prayed he was not among those involved in the accident. Then she prayed for all those who were.

* * *

It was Saturday evening at the end of August of nineteen fifty-eight. Lydia and Dikran had taken the twins to the beach. Lydia marvelled at how much better she had felt since moving to Brighton. She rarely had suffered either asthma attacks or nightmares. Perhaps her improved well-being was due to the sea air, perhaps to the grandchildren. She did not know. She did know she was healthier and happier in Brighton, especially when she was with the twins.

The sea was warm enough for the children to play in the shallows. After, they walked down the pier and enjoyed lunch from the cafeteria. By the time they dropped the children off with their parents, and got home, they were happily tired. They decided to just have a sandwich for dinner. "We can eat in the living room in front of the television, Dikran. I want to watch the quiz show and I'm very tired."

"I'd just like to get the news on BBC before we watch your show," Dikran said. He turned the set on and adjusted the antenna to clear the picture.

"Look Dikran," Lydia pointed to the image that came up. "It's those weirdly dressed boys they now call teddies, you know, like that horrible boy who took our Miriam away."

It was, and what they heard and saw was shocking. There were on-going race riots in the Notting Hill area of London. The announcer started by stating calmly that a mob of about four hundred white youth, presumed to be far-right groups, including Teddy boys, were vandalizing and attacking those in the Caribbean community.

"They are throwing petrol bombs and milk bottles," the announcer said. "It is reported that some have butcher knives and iron bars."

"Dikran," Lydia was shaking, "what is going on? Will there never be any peace? Must people always fight those who are different? Do you know why this is happening, Dikran?"

"I read in the newspaper a couple of days ago that there were tensions in that part of London." He replied. "The way I understand it is that after the war, the government encouraged a lot of black people from the Caribbean to move to England."

"Why would they do that?" Lydia interrupted.

"Because there weren't enough men to fill all the jobs. Remember Lydia, a lot of men got killed in the war. Think about all the re-building and repairs that had to be done. You remember all the bombed-out buildings in London—and of course there are some here too, and in other parts of England. Someone has to fix them, and then there's all the other jobs with no one to take them."

"So, it was a good thing they came then, wasn't it?" Lydia was puzzled.

"It should have been, and I s'pose it kinda is. But here's what seems to have happened. Most the newcomers settled in the same area of Notting Hill—not a great area, but all they could afford. There's been a lot of poverty, crime, and violence around there, Lydia, and there's a shortage of housing."

"But why attack them? I remember when I first moved to London, a lot of our neighbours refused to speak to me. Some even called me names, but they never attacked me."

"Well Lydia, some say it's because there's not enough housing for everyone and so they're just fighting over resources—but I think the real reason is that these violent white men are just racists."

At that moment, Dikran's explanation was supported by pictures of rioting men holding up signs which read "Keep Britain White."

"These are believed to be members of a neo-Nazi political party," the announcer said.

"All my life, Dikran, all my life, there is violence and hatred. Violence and hatred. Why does God allow it? Why aren't people kinder to each other, help each other like the Bible teaches us? Turn it off Dikran. I don't want to hear anymore. It's too awful. I think I'm just going to go to bed."

Lydia went from the living room to the bottom of the staircase that led to their bedroom when she thought she heard a knock at the door. She stopped and listened. She heard a louder and more persistent knocking.

"Dikran," she whispered, "should we open the door? It's a strange time for a visitor." There was more knocking.

"I'll go Lydia." Dikran said. "It sounds like it's urgent."

Dikran opened the door. There was a moment of silence and then he called, "Lydia, you'd better come."

With the news item on the attack fresh in her mind, Lydia was worried. She went quickly to the door. She looked and thought she was imagining what she saw. On the doorstep stood her daughter, Miriam. Beside her was the cutest little boy Lydia had ever seen. He had a mass of black curls and large hazel eyes. He reminded Lydia of her brother, Luke. The boy was holding Miriam's hand with one hand, and with the other, he held onto one arm of an obviously well-loved and well-worn teddy bear.

"Hello mum. I'm home."

"Are you my grandma?" asked a tired voice.

45

Her worries and tiredness forgotten, Lydia could not contain her joy. She enveloped Miriam in a tight hug, and then the child. She could not stop hugging and caressing them.

"This is Noah" Miriam said. "You always told us about Noah and his ark, remember mum. I always thought that was a cute name. So, here he is, my Noah. Your grandson."

"I'm four," Noah announced proudly.

Dikran reminded Lydia that they were all still standing at the door.

They sat around the kitchen table while Lydia heated left-over cabbage dolmas that she had in the refrigerator. Noah suggested they should have some cake. With Miriam's permission, Lydia gave him a large slice of an almond loaf she had baked the day before. After they ate, Miriam asked if they could go to sleep and talk the next day. They had had a long journey, she explained, and were exhausted.

"Teddy is tired too." Noah added.

Noah slept late. Miriam, Lydia, and Dikran lingered over a relaxed Sunday morning breakfast. Lydia had thousands of questions for Miriam, but she restrained herself and let Miriam tell her own story. She had loved Canada, Miriam told them. She had thought about staying there permanently, but two things had led to her return. One was Noah.

Once he was no longer an infant, she realized it would be good for him to be in contact with his family. The photos of the twins had been particularly compelling. Miriam realized how much she was missing. She recalled how, as a child, she had envied her peers who had cousins, aunts, uncles, and grandparents. As a teenager, with little knowledge of her ancestry, she had constantly questioned her identity. She did not want Noah to experience the lack of connectedness and roots that she had. Noah, she had decided, would live close to his extended family.

"But why didn't you tell us about Noah?" Lydia asked.

"I don't really know," Miriam replied. "At first, I was just angry about everything, and then it seemed weird to tell you I had a child. I knew you'd want to see him, and I wasn't ready to come home, and I couldn't imagine you coming all the way to Canada. I knew I would bring Noah home one day."

The second thing that had precipitated her return, she explained, was Johnny.

"He turned out to be a real jerk," she said, "not at all the guy I thought he was."

She described things between them as being okay until Noah was born. Then he started staying out late with his male friends. They would hang out at bars, Miriam told her parents, and gradually he spent more and more of his earnings on beer and cigarettes and gave her less for groceries.

"Sometimes I had to beg him for money to buy food for us," she said, "and he'd say he didn't have enough. But it got a lot worse." She found out through a mutual friend that he was having an affair with an eighteen-year-old neighbour. She confronted him and he laughed at her.

"He said I'd got fat after the baby and he no longer wanted me."

"You look just fine, Miriam." Lydia interjected.

"Yeah, mum. I didn't know what to do for a long time, so I just kinda looked after Noah and sat around feeling miserable. I didn't want to confront him or the kid he was sleeping with. I thought of talking to her parents, but they'd always been real unfriendly. But then I had a brilliant idea. I started watching some of the other kids in the neighbourhood so their mums could go to work or whatever. Johnny didn't even know I was doing it. He wasn't ever there when the kids were. Actually, he was hardly home at all anymore. Anyway, I put all the money aside—actually, I hid it—'til I had enough to buy passage home for me and Noah. And here I am."

"Does he know where you are?" Dikran asked.

"Are you getting a divorce" Lydia asked.

"No, he doesn't know where I am," Miriam replied. "I didn't tell him where we were going, and I made sure to leave nothing behind that would let him figure it out. I left behind a couple of addresses of friends so that he'd think I'd gone to them. They've agreed to refuse to talk to him. He probably won't care, anyway. And, mum, I didn't even need a divorce before I came back. Turned out that because we'd only sorta got married on the ship, we were never registered as married in Canada, and probably not here either. I know I've disappointed you, mum and dad, but this is who I am now. I'm a single mother. But me and Noah, we're going to be okay. I'll show you."

Lydia noticed that Miriam was looking increasingly distressed as she told her story and by the end, there were tears running down her face. They were tears of joy that Miriam had overcome her challenges and had come home with her son. Before either Lydia or Dikran could say anything more, they heard Noah calling for his mother. Miriam ran upstairs and brought him down for some breakfast.

While Noah was having a bowl of cereal, Lydia phoned Leon and Dalita to tell them the news and to invite them all to dinner that night. She thanked God, not for the first time, that she had a phone. Through the afternoon, while Miriam helped Lydia prepare dinner, she talked about her hopes for the future. What she really wanted and was hoping for, she told Lydia, was to go to university and study to become a teacher.

"I remember mum, you used to talk about how much you loved teaching the orphans in Aleppo. You always made it sound like it was just a lot of fun. And now I'm hearing the same stuff from my friend Johnna." She had, she explained, stayed in touch with her friend Johnna, who had become a teacher at a junior school. Johnna was happily married to another teacher.

"Just like you used to say when I was little, Johnna says it's great being a teacher," Miriam said. "She loves the kids and is so glad we didn't go through with our teenage plans to be airplane stewardesses. I think I want to do teaching too. I know I've grown up a lot, mum. I want to be successful and be a good mother and teacher like you. And maybe it's not too late to be a good daughter." She smiled at Lydia.

Lydia was thrilled and offered to look after Noah while Miriam went to classes.

The dinner that night was joyous. The twins and Noah played happily together. Miriam was thrilled to reunite with her brother, and to meet Dalita, Gemma, and Emin. Lydia had never been happier, and Dikran had never been prouder. They decided that since the next day was Sunday and neither Leon nor Dalita were on call, they would prepare a picnic and take the children to the park.

That night, Lydia bathed Noah and tucked him into bed. She asked him if he knew the story of Noah and the ark.

"I'm Noah," he replied. "I don't know what's a ark."

Lydia told him the story, encouraging him to participate by making the sounds of the animals that Noah was leading into the ark. She realized it was not an ideal way to get him to settle down to sleep, but they were both having too much fun to be sensible, she decided. After the story ended, she asked the question she used to ask Luke.

"What animals would you put in the ark?" she asked Noah.

"Dinosaurs," he said loudly and without hesitation. Lydia immediately became her eight-year-old self and felt the pangs of loss of her brother. She recovered quickly when Noah said, "Good night, Grandma. I love you."

"I have a treat for you, Noah." Lydia told him a few days later. You and I are going to have an adventure and go on a train to London and—."

"What's London?" Noah interrupted her.

"It's a big, big city, Noah. But there we are going to go to a museum and see some dinosaurs."

"Real live dinosaurs?' Noah sounded astonished.

"Well, they're not alive Noah, but they are real."

One happy grandmother and one very excited little boy arrived at the Natural History Museum's dinosaur exhibit after an hour-long train ride, which they both enjoyed. Noah was overwhelmed by the size of the dinosaurs. He stood comparing his own leg with one of the front legs of a brontosaurus. Lydia read the sign to him. "It says here that the brontosaurus can weigh up to fifty thousand pounds and measure seventy-four feet from head to tail."

A security guard who had been standing close by came over and told Lydia that they had just missed a talk by the paleontologist. "But if this little boy has any questions, he's right there. He knows all about dinosaurs and he likes talking to the children." He pointed to a man who was talking to a little girl. The man was standing a short distance in front of Lydia, with his back to her. Lydia sensed something familiar about him although she was unsure what it was. The security guard walked up to him and said something.

The paleontologist turned. Seeing his face, Lydia had a flash of recognition. Lydia paled, and shook as she read his name tag: Dr. L Zakarian.

"Luke?" There was a moment of silence. Then, a broad smile lit Dr. Zakarian's face. He held his arms out.

"Lydia!"

With tears of joy running down their faces, they clasped each other. Noah and the dinosaurs looked on.

Epilogue

Every seat in the auditorium was taken. The plenary session was about to begin. The dean of the university stood at the microphone ready to introduce the keynote speaker.

"Good morning," she began. "As many of you may know, today, April 24, 1965, is the fiftieth anniversary of the Armenian Genocide. That makes it so very appropriate that this year's winner of the PhD dissertation award is a young woman who not only has produced seminal and ground-breaking work on genocide survivors, but who herself is Armenian. Without further ado, ladies and gentlemen, I am delighted to present this year's winner, Dr. Miriam Vartounian."

"Hoorah, mum!" The shout from the boy in the front row of the audience brought forth laughter and applause. The applause was loudest and most prolonged among those sitting around him—Lydia and Dikran, Luke, Leon, Dalita and the twins, the Krikorians, Eva and Raffi, and even Sarah who had come from Marseille. Lydia, who was bursting with pride, felt as though she finally had a real extended and loving family. Miriam stepped up to the microphone and began her talk.

"Good morning and thank you all for this honour. Seven years ago, I decided to go to university and study to become a teacher. I could not have done so without the incredible support of my parents, Dikran and Lydia Vartounian. Not only did they agree to support me for the three-year education program, but they also continued to encourage and support me as my interests and ambitions evolved and my years of study grew longer, and longer, and longer. Thank you and I love you." She paused and smiled at her family members. She continued as the applause died down.

"My interests, and I assume my family history, led me to the study of the effects of genocide on the girl-child. This morning I am going to present a summary of my research."

"I conducted multiple interviews with fifty-three Armenian women who were genocide survivors. Each is currently living in Southern England. My mother and my brother's mother-in-law were among them. Every one of my subjects had been a child in Armenia between the ages of six and twelve in nineteen fifteen. They all emigrated to England as adults, either directly from the Middle East or after spending some time in Marseille, France. So, these women represent a generation who experienced genocide and loss when they were children. Then, as adults, they went through immigration, adaptation to new lands, language and culture, and the horrors of the Second World War. They are truly a remarkable group." Miriam paused and then stressed her point. "Remarkable women. When I analyzed the interview data, four major themes emerged. I will summarize them today. I'm not going into great detail because I want to leave a lot of time for questions and discussion and also, if you'll forgive the plug, I have a book coming out on the topic—it's called *The women of Armenia: genocide survivors tell their stories.*"

"So, the four themes."

"First, every one of the women who I interviewed revealed an overwhelming sense of ongoing victimization. This was in part due to their sense of loss in childhood—a loss that continued. They lost their family members, their homeland, their language, and their culture. Many had also lost their childhood innocence in ways that had profound lifelong consequences—the experience of rape was common. These losses were experienced internally as an overall lack of safety, of predictability, and of personal identity. Everything that had been predictable, safe, and familiar was gone. There was no returning. They could get nothing back." Miriam paused and took a sip of water. She noticed that her mother was looking uncomfortable.

"Their sense of victimization was also due to and intensified by the lack of acknowledgement of, and accountability for, the genocide. The denial of the genocide by the Turkish government, that there has been no accountability or justice for what happened has been hurtful and has made it harder to resolve the grief they have felt and continue to feel.

Why, they wonder, has there been no acknowledgement, no apology, no reparation? It is belittling, demeaning. Does it mean as a people and as individuals that they don't matter? Recall, as more than one pointed out in the interviews, what Hitler said in 1939: who, after all, speaks today of the annihilation of the Armenians." Miriam paused and looked at the audience for a moment before continuing. Her voice betrayed her passion.

"Indeed, we might ask, who today even knows of the Armenians? Most of the women I talked to said that when they met people and introduced themselves as Armenians, they were met with puzzlement. And I add, my experience has been the same. Few, it seemed to them, and to me, even know there are such people, let alone their history. This lack of recognition, this lack of accountability, clearly has a long-term effect on survivors. So how have they responded? This brings me to my second common finding." Another pause, another sip of water while she checked the expression and posture of her mother. Lydia was sitting stiffly upright.

"The most common response was repression—or attempts at repression of the memories that continue to haunt them. Life histories, the traumatic events of their childhoods and adolescence were not discussed. Not mentioned. They were taboo subjects. It was as though there was no past, no personal history. Their children's questions remained unanswered. Some would express themselves in letters to friends, but not in the family and never to their children."

"When I talked with them more, I discovered two basic reasons for this. One was concern for their children. Many expressed fears that any disclosure of their past—if they talked of the horrors they had experienced—would have a negative impact on their children. So, they tried to spare them through silence, to bury their past, to protect their children in the present. A second reason, and one which seems more dominant, was more a need to protect themselves. Talking about their experiences and allowing their feelings to emerge were too emotionally challenging."

"The third major commonality was how the repression affected them. The problem with trying to repress trauma is that it has a profound impact on mental and physical well-being. Traumatic experiences need to be dealt with. Everyone of those I interviewed suffered from flashbacks and nightmares in which the traumatic incidents of their childhood were relived, over and over and over. Most also talked of low self-worth, ongoing fatigue, depression, anxiety, and distrust. Some experienced panic attacks. None had received any professional help for their feelings. But not all was or is negative." Looking at her parents, and noting the tears on Lydia's face, Miriam was glad she was getting to a positive point.

"My fourth finding, and a much happier one, was the incredible level of resilience they exhibited despite the challenges I have summarized. And if you'll forgive a personal note, I think my mother is a powerful example of resilience. She survived the loss of her family, servitude and abuse, orphanage life, emigration, the Second World War and even me." The audience chuckled. "She is truly among the most remarkable of women." The applause continued until Lydia stood and acknowledged the audience. Miriam continued.

"Over and over, the interviews ended with the respondents stressing their successes. Like my mother, they were successful in adapting to England, in learning the language, in working hard, in getting through the war, in raising children, and above all, in maintaining an Armenian community. We'll flourish again, one said. Another said, we Armenians are strong, we're tough. Look at all the important Armenians, all the Armenian actors, athletes, and writers. We're proud of them. They are us. We are all connected. They'll never keep us down. We are grateful to be here and to fit in okay, but we will always be Armenians. The urge to retain cultural identity was strong. Some of you here likely experienced the same pressure to marry an Armenian as I did." Miriam smiled at her mother. The audience laughed. A few nodded knowingly. "Not that it worked."

She continued. "I was going to stop at this point and open the floor for questions, but I want to first talk for a few minutes about where my research is now. You see, I have come to realize that we—the children of the survivors—may also be affected by the genocide. Let me explain what I mean. First, I emphasize here that I have no research on this—I hope to in the future, and I hope others will as well. What I share with you now is based on my experience and informal chats with others whose parents were child genocide survivors."

"I think that many of us feel rather lost. We have never met our extended family. We really know nothing about them. Is there a family history of diabetes, a doctor asked me one day. I don't know, I told him. He was puzzled. Who are we, who were our grandparents, our extended family? Do we still have family somewhere? Many of us don't even really know what our parents or grandparents lived through—we can guess based on what we have learned, but what really happened? How did their experiences shape their parenting, shape us? I don't know to what extent these questions affect our overall mental and physical health and well-being. Maybe not at all. But I know they are there, and they haunt us.

"I now open the floor for questions."

The story of Lydia and her family is a work of fiction. But the historical context and information presented is, to the best of my knowledge, accurate. For the Armenian Genocide, I have drawn from contemporaneous accounts from governments and the media, archival records, and academic research. Thirty-three countries have accepted that during the first world war, the Ottoman Empire, led by the Union and Progress Committee, undertook an act of genocide against Armenians. The Genocide has most recently been recognized by President Biden of the United States (2021). Estimates are that of two million Armenians, between one and one and a half million were killed. Likewise, the incidents described during the Second World War are based on contemporaneous and archival accounts. Further information on all the events described is readily available through numerous books, websites, and historical documents.

An easy to read yet comprehensive summary of the Armenian genocide is the online article *Facing History and Ourselves*, "Genocide under the Cover of War" at https://www.facinghistory.org/resource-library/genocide-under-cover-war

Other useful links include:

University of Minnesota, Holocaust and Genocide Studies - Armenia
https://cla.umn.edu/chgs/holocaust-genocide-education/resource-guides/armenia

History Channel - Armenia
https://www.history.com/topics/world-war-i/armenian-genocide

Armenian National Institute - Sample Archival Documents
https://www.armenian-genocide.org/sampledocs.html

The Armenian Genocide Museum-Institute - Links
http://www.genocide-museum.am/eng/links.php

Links may become outdated or change content. The publisher and author are not responsible for the accuracy or content of these links.

I am indebted to my editor, Tim Covell, for his incredible ability to find all my historical and grammatical errors [ed note: touch wood]. His work has resulted in a product that is much improved from its original draft. I also am grateful to all those who have encouraged me to indulge in my passion for writing and my need to share this story which, although fictional, is based on my mother's childhood and to some extent my own. Always supportive have been my partner Brian, my family, and my friends.

I am also very grateful to all those, friends and strangers, who read and commented (positively that is) on my previous novel *Flipping the Switch*, especially those who wrote reviews. Your interest and your words were profoundly gratifying and encouraging. I am especially grateful to all the historians, archivists, and researchers who documented WWII, the genocide, and the holocaust with such detail and through various media have made their findings accessible. They made this story possible.

Katherine Covell is a developmental psychologist and child right's activist with a long history of academic books and articles. This is her second novel. *Flipping the Switch* was published by Somewhat Grumpy Press in 2021. She lives in Vancouver, British Columbia, Canada.

Lace doily, made by the author's mother.
One-inch coin for scale.